PRESUMPTION OF DEATH

JOY RATCLIFF CAGLE

Strategic Book Publishing and Rights Co.

Strategic Book Publishing and Rights Co.
12620 FM 1960, Suite A4-507
Houston, TX 77065
www.sbpra.com

ISBN: 978-1-62212-979-9

THIS BOOK IS DEDICATED
TO THE GUILTY
AND IN MEMORY OF CARRIE

To Ashley — I'm enjoying
getting to know you!

9-18-14

ACKNOWLEDGEMENTS

THIS BOOK has evolved over many years. During the struggles of research, fact checking, and writing, along with working in the legal field, I have gained a deeper respect and admiration for those among us who strive to make a difference.

I thank the people and organizations who have unselfishly contributed their wisdom and caution. You know who you are and you understand that I cannot name you personally.

The University of West Florida professor who guided me through the strange yet awesome emotions attached to clairvoyant visions, the forensic expert, polygraph detective Brooks who helped me understand how intimidating this test can be by putting me through one, the Sheriff who refused to be a part of corruption, my lawyer friends who are always trying to curb my outspoken opinions, and to my friends and family who walked with me on this leg of my journey.

My daughter for being there. My grandchildren who have christened me as the strangest grandmother in the world, and are anxiously waiting to see if I can really write a good book.

And my husband who has been beside me through joy and pain, hot air balloon rides and ballets. Thank you. I am forever grateful.

BE NOT DECEIVED; GOD IS NOT MOCKED:
FOR WHATSOEVER A MAN SOWETH,
THAT SHALL HE ALSO REAP

Galatians 6:7

CHAPTER ONE

MR. AND MRS. LARRY NOLAND
YOU ARE CORDIALLY INVITED TO A GALA
IN HONOR OF DISTRICT ATTORNEY
DONALD BUTCHER

"Another brainless party for the esteemed district attorney in honor of his recent victory at some trial," Sheri hissed as she read the invitation.

Donald Butcher had an ego the size of infinity and gloating, albeit commonplace, required a professional forum — a party. The Nolands would have to go even if Sheri objected. To do otherwise was considered rude and Larry had a lawyer image to uphold. These were *his* friends and colleagues and one must never disappoint the privileged.

"I hate these damn parties — I hate them," Sheri screamed into the quiet of her home, stomped into the kitchen and threw the invitation to the floor. She did not bother picking it up.

* * * *

"Damn it, Sheridan, hurry up. Get your ass out the door. You always make us late." Larry's voice dripped with indignation.

"I'm coming. All right? Don't be so impatient," she yelled back, started to say something else then caught herself in time, not wanting his anger to flare as it had in recent weeks. They strolled a couple of blocks in silence through the manicured neighborhood and up the illuminated sidewalk to Donald Butcher's impressive

1

Tudor-styled house. Sheri let out a heavy sigh.

All the important people were there — people who knew how to pull strings and get things done their way — the congressmen, the judges, the lawyers, the politicians, the business executives. It amazed Sheri that each time a social function took place the same group of people attended; always the prominent Southern boys, cloaked in respectability but malignant to the core. Outsiders were never allowed.

One of the small groups that were huddled in corners discussing boring topics included Judge Henry Johnson, one of the district's most prominent federal judges. Several lawyers stood laughing and reciting their latest adventures in court, exaggerating the facts to enhance their image.

Like a hawk eyeing its prey, Judge Johnson studied Sheri as she meandered through the house. He appreciated beautiful women and Sheri was exquisite, poised, tall and willowy. He thought about how Sheri disturbed him in a way he did not like or understand as he watched her, and even though she was always pleasant to him, there was something in her manner as she smiled suggesting that she did not approve of him or anyone else present.

Sheri circulated through the dining room pausing at the table to sample hors d'oeuvres, listening to bits and pieces of conversations resonating from all directions.

"Don, your closing statement was remarkable. Let's have a toast to the illustrious district attorney."

"Judge, would you do the honors?"

"Congressman, do you think the district attorney worthy of your blessing?" Everyone laughed, knowing the district attorney was the congressman's golden boy. Donald Butcher was good-looking, aggressive and always confident in his decisions. Each time he won a case he not only made himself look good, but he enhanced Congressman Wise's reputation as well. The congressman was grooming Donald Butcher for rapid advancement in the political arena knowing he would serve them well. Their private, joint acquisitions would make them a fortune, and once the district attorney was placed in the U.S. Senate, nothing could hold them back.

Sheri caught whispers drifting from the hallway.

"The shipment's due in next week. Everything's been arranged and I don't anticipate any problems."

"Has Don taken care of the escorts?"

"Doesn't he always?"

"Johnson has assured everyone that this will put us over the top."

"What about the new associates?"

"We'll have no problems from Noland I assure you. He's bought and paid for, loyal as a puppy. This shipment will net us millions and then we'll see who has the power in this state. Our esteemed governor will only wish he had our connections."

Sheri strained to hear more, conscious of other people wandering around. Intentionally eavesdropping now, her senses were attuned to even the slightest insinuation. *These men are lawyers and politicians. This is not a case or a political victory they're discussing. Either of those could produce millions of dollars but shipments? Escorts? What are they talking about? And what are they saying about my husband?*

"Distribution will be handled in the usual manner."

"Will Don and his boys provide complete protection this time?"

"Has he ever let us down?" Muffled laughter followed.

"The trucking line is the best defense yet. So happy that our new friend could join us this evening and share his wisdom. We must congratulate the firm on its discretionary tactics. Best move we ever made having him become a colleague rather than a client." The men laughed again and with raised glasses toasted each other as they made their way back to the dining room to join the others.

Sheri recoiled in disbelief as the context of the conversation sank in. *Stay calm and smile; walk away, look like a guest having a good time. You cannot know of the conversation you just overheard.*

* * * *

"Goodnight. We had a splendid time and again congratulations, Don. As always you scored a fine victory for our side." Sheri and Larry said their farewells and ambled down the quiet street.

Larry had chosen this particular area of town for their first home because he thought it was suitable for a person of distinction. As they made their way home, the fragrance of sweet, sensual honeysuckle wrapped itself around Sheri, and a soothing breeze caressed her face, somewhat easing tension from the disturbing night. The temperature had dropped to a pleasant sixty degrees. A few years earlier this would have been a romantic end to a wonderful evening, instead Sheri, exhausted and wanting nothing more than to go home and straight to bed, was shaken to her core by what she'd overheard. Tomorrow after a good night's sleep she would discuss the matter with Larry. They had mentioned his name in an unscrupulous manner and the implications were frightening. She must have misunderstood.

Larry was distant and moody tonight, and Sheri realized that his withdrawal had worsened the past few months. She felt excluded from his priorities, but justified his behavior as stress related to overwork at the firm. Associates were required to bill hundreds of hours per month and their performance was rated accordingly. As a rule Larry worked twelve to sixteen-hour days six days a week.

Passing by the Georgian home of a distinguished surgeon, Sheri thought about the large cash bonuses Larry had received from the firm. He instructed her to either spend the cash or invest it, but never deposit it into their checking or saving accounts. Whenever she questioned him about the considerable amounts of money, he explained that they were bonuses given after cases were settled, perks of an exceptional firm and non-taxable when paid in cash. It seemed suspicious to Sheri, nevertheless time after time Larry assured her it was an acceptable, legal practice in respectable law firms.

Lost in thought she was going through the front door before she even realized they were home.

"Larry, I'm really exhausted. Maybe we can have breakfast together in the morning before you leave for the office," Sheri whispered as she hugged him. He studied her face with concern, smiled, kissed her cheek and said goodnight. In the safety of their bedroom, Sheri dropped her clothes on the floor, climbed into their antique, king-sized bed and turned out the lights sighing. Her thoughts running rampant she finally drifted off into a troubled sleep, unaware that Larry never joined her in their bed.

* * * *

Sheri had glanced through the mail a few days earlier hopeful to receive the results of her bar exam. She had studied night and day to pass the bar and her patience was exhausted waiting on the outcome. Larry, already a practicing lawyer in a very prestigious law firm in the small town of Canton, Georgia, shadowed Congressman Alan Wise, a former partner in the firm. The congressman was a very outspoken figure, and his liberal opinions shocked other politicians and voters throughout the state, yet the masses continued to re-elect him.

Rumors lurked around the congressman. No one in Canton dared voice his or her thoughts about him out loud for fear of retaliation. The South was well known for its prominent 'good ole boys' network, and the congressman in his powerful behind-the-scenes role as leader of this network, could cause one to lose a job, a home, a place in society and perhaps even a life. He was a man privately feared but publicly respected. Those who knew him well dared not say a word against him or cross him in any way.

Sheri knew in her bones that when she became a practicing lawyer it would create more discord in her marriage. Her views on everything opposed her husband's. She did not share his political views, his social affiliations, least of all his deification of the congressman. She vowed that after she became a lawyer she would implement changes in this corrupt legal world, changes that really mattered. She abhorred inequity, political or otherwise. Sheri had already learned more than she ever wanted to know about injustice watching her husband grovel at the feet of the senior partners of his law firm. Always too eager to please he appeared to be no more than an educated errand boy but Larry would never see himself through her eyes. His inflated ego controlled him as much as the partners did, and he was on his way to the top no matter what he had to do to get there.

Larry was demanding; his needs, his desires, his feelings always came before Sheri's. She could never quite define what she saw in his intense, ebony eyes that frightened her. Could it be a mere reflection of her own insecurities?

They met in law school when both were criminal justice students and in an odd sort of way, Larry's always-in-control attitude impressed her then. She had seen something, a haunting quality in his dark eyes, a deep inner turmoil that intrigued her. He made her feel desirable yet unworthy at the same time, an explosive combination. He awakened passions in her she never knew existed, but was jealous beyond control demanding all of her attention and time. For a while his jealousy was flattering. Forceful in his pursuit of Sheri, Larry exhausted her defenses until she agreed to marry him. His strong determination intrigued her — it was one of the things she had most loved about him in the beginning. Now, that same determination disturbed her as she watched him becoming cold and calculating, drifting further and further away. Sheri could never allow anyone to know how unhappy she had become. Larry's behavior frightened her at times, however she was only beginning to understand to what extent.

CHAPTER TWO

"Good morning, baby. Coffee?" Sheri asked as she poured Larry a cup.

"Did you enjoy the party last night?" Not waiting for a response she plunged ahead before she lost her nerve.

"Some of the conversations I heard were a bit confusing even coming from that group."

"Yeah, it was interesting. Judge Johnson always makes me laugh. What conversation was confusing?" he asked raising a questioning eyebrow. "You need to get to the point, Sheri, I'm going to be late for work if I don't hurry."

Knowing that she should not be having this conversation with Larry, she couldn't seem to stop herself and blurted out, "I heard your name mentioned several times when Judge Johnson was talking with the D.A. about money and shipments. He said you were bought and paid for and he didn't have to worry about you. What was he talking about, Larry? What have you done?" Sheri waited holding her breath.

Larry's ebony eyes explored her face making her uncomfortable. He showed no anger, was not startled, just strangely calm. Smiling he said, "I have no idea what you are talking about, Sheri. Maybe they had a few too many drinks. You need to go to work as well before you're late. Let's hope you get the bar results today and at long last you'll be a real lawyer."

He placed a peck on her cheek and was out the door. Sheri believed she heard him mumble before getting into his Jeep, "You stupid, stupid bitch."

* * * *

eighty-one degrees and no rain in sight, the air was suffocat-
ing even at nine in the morning, surpassing records of past Septem-
bers. A dull brown crawled across the veins of green leaves as they
dehydrated and curled on the trees.

Gripped by fear and weary from lack of sleep, Sheri fumbled
with her keys trying to lock the front door of their house. The
unbearable heat combined with her movement produced crashing
waves of pain across her forehead. With growing alarm her eyes
darted around making sure Larry's Jeep was nowhere in sight as she
bolted toward Linda's waiting Camaro.

Out of the corner of her eye she noticed a crow gawking at her
from its perch in the trees. Its mere presence caused shivers the
length of her spine, and she felt a sense of gloom creeping over her.
What the hell is wrong with me? Now crows are making me crazy? She
remembered some folklore about crows and their connection to the
afterlife, but the memory couldn't quite surface before she heard
Linda's spirited voice.

"Good morning," Linda greeted her with an infectious grin. "I
can't believe you gave in at last and want to go see the psychic."

"It's not that I *want* to see her — it's need. She might be able to
help me sort out some quirky things in my life and besides, it gives
you an excuse to spend time with me." She smiled.

"Well, you're going to love her and it is an experience you'll never
forget," Linda said with a teasing wink as she drove out of the circle
driveway headed north toward Highway 5.

Sheri's friends visited the psychic for entertainment when they
were bored, but Sheri had never joined them. Always skeptical of
the unknown, she would never have gone to a self-professed psychic
but now she was afraid, haunted by bits of overheard conversation.
And on this day she knew there was no one else who could help her.

Sheridan Hilliard Noland and Linda Fox became friends in college and continued the kinship through Sheri's trying years at
Emory Law School. Enthusiasm was Linda's driving force. A former

college cheerleader, she retained an energetic interest in every aspect of life. Long, blond curls bounced over her shoulders as she laughed at Sheri's reluctance to admit she wanted, rather than needed, to visit the psychic.

"Are you all right? You're too quiet."

"I have a lot on my mind and I'm tired. I didn't sleep well last night." Forlorn and distant Sheri gazed out the window not wanting Linda to see the fear shadowing her face.

"If psychics really have a sixth sense about things perhaps she can tell me what to do. I'm sorry I can't share this problem with you, but thanks for taking me." Sheri paused for a moment searching her friend's face for understanding, and then turned to stare out the window not waiting for a reply.

They drove on the winding two-lane highway thirty-five miles across the mountain in eerie silence while music on the radio went unnoticed. Sheri's mind retraced last night's conversation. *Noland bought and paid for — shipments — the trucking company's allegiance with the law firm — millions of dollars — the district attorney — the governor.*

Driving into the yard of the weathered, wood-framed house Linda announced in disbelief, "There must be at least twenty people waiting to see her."

Standing in the psychic's yard, sitting on her porch steps, and crouched in parked cars were people from different walks of life, each waiting on a turn with the psychic known only as Grammy. Ever vigilant Grammy locked the door behind each visitor peering out half-shaded windows. Enormous elm trees with far-reaching appendages shrouded the structure and concealed it from other houses. Linda and Sheri waited in the car watching Grammy summon one person after another into the house. Some stayed longer and came out smiling with relief, while others fled sobbing.

"Sheri, what's going on? You are distressed beyond belief. I'm your best friend remember? Can't you talk to me?" Linda probed.

"I'm sorry. This is not something I can talk about right now. I promise to tell you later."

"Is it Larry? I know the two of you are at odds most of the time these days. He's such a pompous ass."

Linda had no respect for Larry and his God-complex and she did not like the way he treated Sheri. In her opinion, Sheri was more intelligent than Larry and he was jealous.

"Can we open the windows? It's sweltering." Sheri did not want to discuss this subject.

Linda lowered the windows, leaned back in her seat and closed her eyes. Guns 'N' Roses' new hit song played on the radio unnoticed. She respected her friend's decision to tell her nothing before seeing Grammy, but she hoped Sheri would share afterward. Sheri massaged her temples trying to remove the thoughts that threatened to crush her. The humidity made the heat more unbearable as the day grew longer, and the scorching sun radiated overhead. Still they waited.

An analytical mind — logical — factual — black and white; those were the ideals that defined Sheri Noland. Visiting a psychic was not consistent with those traits. She never would have made it through law school without possessing a predominate left-brain, but now rational thought was buried in the recesses of her mind. Motivated by crippling fear she sat in Linda's car a different Sheri — one she no longer recognized, a Sheri who did not seem to possess even one single logical brain cell. A Sheri who was terrified.

She watched. Only three people left before she could talk with Grammy and end the tortuous thoughts swirling in her head. Four sweltering hours had passed since they arrived.

The old psychic opened the front door and beckoned with a wave of her gnarly hand for Sheri to enter her house. Forcing her legs to move, she dragged herself up the porch steps holding onto the splintered banister and entered the house behind Grammy. Sheri studied the dank, old people smelling room afraid to move.

Tables thick with dust were cluttered with knick-knacks; yellowing newspapers and magazines of years past were stacked knee-high on the floor. Spider webs hung from the ceiling corners. Closed doors prevented access to other areas of the house.

A landmark in the small community both admired and feared, Grammy was a mystery and oftentimes the recipient of cruel pranks. Although physically frail, her mind commanded respect. She was older than most of the historic stone churches in the area. Years of excessive physical wear had curled her spine forward forcing her to use a walking cane. Thinning, silver hair pulled tight over her scalp was held by a child's barrette emphasizing her aging face. Her craggy face reminded Sheri of the apple dolls she had made as a student in Mrs. Martin's sixth grade class, and she couldn't help but smile at the memory.

Grammy pointed to two chairs facing each other in a corner of the small room. Worn from years of use, the seat cushions were threadbare with stuffing protruding from torn seams. Sheri wondered how many others had sat on these chairs consumed with fear as she did now, waiting for an answer. Unable to dispel a sense of doom Grammy dead bolted the door, watching through half shaded windows until she was satisfied no one was coming in. After the longest time she sat down opposite Sheri. Without speaking she studied Sheri's face through opaque blue eyes that seemed to not only pierce one's soul, but penetrated far beyond.

"Why are you here child?" she whispered never taking her eyes from Sheri's.

"I'm not sure," Sheri whispered back. "I'm afraid. I don't know what to do. I overheard a conversation at a party last night. My husband — my husband's name was mentioned. I tried to ask him — he refused to tell me anything. He was — strange."

Grammy took Sheri's trembling hands into her own fragile ones. Raised blue veins on the top of Grammy's hands made the wrinkled flesh appear translucent. Through glazed eyes she continued to study Sheri's face. Grammy did not speak; she did not move. Eternal moments passed before she leaned closer, let go of Sheri's hands and mouthed the words, "Child, you're in danger. Go at once to a safe place. Not home. Tell no one where you're going. Go!"

She wrung her withered hands. "Don't go home. Don't go home!"

Before Sheri could rise from the chair or ask why she should not go home, Grammy grasped her face letting out a piercing moan. Startled Sheri jerked away and stumbled over the stacks of paper on the floor trying to reach the door. She fumbled with the door lock until it opened, then fled across the porch, down the steps and into the yard almost falling, not looking back.

Grammy bolted the door behind her allowing no one else to enter even though several people were waiting. Her blood-curdling moan could still be heard as Sheri dove into Linda's car. *What had the old woman seen?*

"My God, Sheri are you all right?" Linda asked. "You're trembling and your face is white as death. What did that old witch say to you?"

"Drive, Linda. Please just get me out of here."

Linda sped out of the yard leaving behind a trail of dust, and did not slow down until she was halfway across the mountain.

Sheri stared ahead fighting to slow her breath and ease the pounding in her chest. She did not want Linda to see the terror in her eyes and she could not explain what she didn't know.

"I can't talk about it," she gasped. "I'm scared, all right? I'll tell you after I've had time to comprehend what she said. Just be my friend and understand please," Sheri pleaded.

Pack my clothes. Pick up my car. Get cash. Leave Larry a note. No! Grammy said not to go home. Just leave and tell no one. She said I was in danger. How? Why didn't she tell me?

Shaking with such intensity that she was sure her bones would shatter, Sheri forced her back against the seat trying to steady herself. Without conscious effort her eyes began to close and thoughts of Larry, last night's party, and the events of the past week replayed in her mind. Linda headed back to Sheri's house — the very place Grammy insisted she not go.

* * * *

Abruptly brought back to the present, Sheri jolted upright with a startled expression as Linda remarked, "Now what's Larry doing home at this hour?" She pulled into the driveway directly behind his Jeep.

Without waiting for Sheri's answer, she continued. "Okay, now I understand. The two of you did have a fight. That's why you went to see Grammy and now he's home to make up again. Glad I'm not in your shoes. I won't come in."

She blew Sheri a kiss but the expression on her face remained one of concern. "If you need me — call."

Sheri got out of the car while her mind screamed for her to get back in and have Linda drive her far away. Instead she waved to her best friend, watched her car drive out of the driveway and felt an unexpected sadness. Logic and facts, not psychic gibberish controlled her life, but Larry should not be home at this time of the day. Something *was* wrong, very wrong.

"What are you doing home this early?" she asked as he met her at the front door.

"I called your office and the receptionist said you were home sick. I thought I'd come see about you. We didn't have any critical deadlines today so I told my secretary I had a dentist appointment." He studied Sheri as if he could see through her. "Where have you and Linda been? Are you really sick?"

"No, just tired. We went into town to do a little shopping but didn't find anything worth buying," she lied. "I thought getting out might make me feel better."

Now she would have to wait until morning to leave. Sheri was more frightened than she had been at Grammy's and she knew she would have to be aware of Larry's every move. He'd never come home early to see about her even when she was sick. Without a doubt she knew she should have listened to Grammy. She should have had Linda take her anywhere but home. Grammy had scared the life out of her and she did not have time to think about another place to go.

Sheri poured herself a glass of iced tea and sat down on the sofa across the room from Larry where she felt safer. She had not eaten all day because the thought of food made her nauseous.

"You remember the insurance case I was telling you about the other day?" Larry asked.

Lost in tormenting thoughts, Sheri didn't respond.

"Sheridan, you must pay attention if you're ever going to learn anything. Didn't they teach you in law school the importance of listening skills?"

"I'm sorry, sweetheart, it's been a long day and I'm not feeling well at all. What did you say?" She tried to listen but her mind kept going back to Grammy's warning.

"This will be one of my greatest cases," Larry said. "One that will make other attorneys take notice. I've got the bastard for insurance fraud."

Larry strutted around the room. "Damn, I'm good. He'll never know what happened when I'm through with him. Too bad Sheri you'll never get the opportunity to try a case."

Only half-listening to Larry's boasting Sheri caught his last remark. It startled her back to full attention and fear widened her eyes. In an attempt to disguise the shock of what sounded like a threat, she raised the glass of iced tea to her lips, got off the sofa and hurried back to the kitchen. She inhaled with control letting the air leave her lungs without sound, trying to delay her reaction to his words.

"What did you say, Larry? About not ever trying a case?"

"Damn, Sheri face the facts. You'll never be as good a lawyer as I am. You're not aggressive enough. You don't have what it takes to get in there and fight to win. You should have been a schoolteacher like your mother, that's more your style. Whipping little kids into shape," he mockingly said.

"You're not as clever as you think, Larry." She was too exhausted to argue with him and too scared to think.

Larry felt a sense of accomplishment knowing he had made her feel inferior. Satisfied with himself, he turned on the television and sat down to watch a preview of the Tennessee/Georgia football game, dismissing her with his silence.

* * * *

Evening approached as they sat down to a light dinner on the patio even though the heat was still oppressive. Mixed, green salad topped with cold, sliced baked chicken and French bread was all Sheri had been capable of preparing. Her stomach churned each time she tried to take a bite, and when Larry questioned her lack of appetite, she blamed it on the heat. She feared talking about the overheard conversation at the party would send him into a rage and he was not going to bring it up.

As they made small talk after dinner Sheri began to relax a little. She was enjoying the scented, autumn night air and Larry was his charming self again.

The old psychic didn't say Larry was the danger. It could be someone from the party or no one. Stop these insane thoughts and irrational fears, Sheri.

He caressed her face with his forefinger, but she noticed he had an odd smile on his face.

"Honey, let's take a drive. I have a surprise for you."

"It's almost ten thirty, Larry and I'm exhausted. I just want to go to bed. Can't it wait until tomorrow?"

"Ah, come on, baby, it will only take a few minutes. I know you'll love it," said Larry. "It's my way of making up to you for being so irritable earlier today. I didn't mean what I said. You'll make a fine lawyer someday."

He stroked her hair and kissed her cheek knowing she would not refuse him. Too tired to argue she agreed to go, and walked across the sidewalk ahead of Larry. He opened the Jeep door and helped her in.

With an exaggerated, slow, Southern drawl that always charmed Sheri, he said, "Baby, since it's a surprise I don't want you to see where we're going. Let's put this scarf over your eyes so you'll really be surprised."

"Larry, this is ridiculous. I don't want my eyes covered. Can't we just go?"

"It will make the surprise more fun if we do it this way. Lighten up, Sheri, you're in such a bad mood." Larry ignored her pleas and began to cover her eyes with the scarf, tying it behind her head knowing she would not try to remove it. She was childlike when she was very tired and he knew if he insisted she would give in. He knew her well.

"I forgot my wallet. Can't drive without my license. Just sit there and wait for me while I run back into the house. I'll be one minute."

As the door clicked shut Grammy's words exploded inside Sheri's head. Tentacles of fear squeezed the air from her lungs. *Don't go home. Tell no one where you're going.* Yet she remained in the Jeep quietly waiting for her husband, disbelieving. She would not be afraid of Larry because he could never physically hurt her. Trust and love. Her marriage was built upon these qualities. This was just a silly little-boy game he was playing and her imagination was running wild. Besides, Grammy had spooked her. Crazy old woman. She never should have gone to see her. Sheri heard the door open and shut. She heard Larry's quiet laughter over the sound of the engine and the Jeep began to move.

At eleven forty-five that night Larry drove back into his driveway alone. He looked around making sure none of his neighbors saw him. Once inside the house he poured a double scotch and threw it down his throat savoring the burn. He had cooperated and shown his loyalty without hesitation, now he needed to sleep. The next few days were going to be difficult ones, and he must be mindful and in control of his actions at all times. No mistakes. He set the clock alarm for three A.M. and stretched out on the sofa fully clothed.

* * * *

Three houses up the dark street from the Noland residence, a female driver let Daniel Spicer out of her car at twelve thirty. Without delay Spicer made his way on foot through the trees to Larry's Jeep parked in the driveway. As promised the keys were in the ignition and he drove the Jeep away leaving the sleeping neighborhood.

* * * *

The clock alarm blared startling Larry from a disturbed sleep. He slammed his hand over it knocking it to the floor. He tried to get the kinks out of his limbs by stretching, and needing to walk he went to the window to peer out into the darkness. He let out a relieved sigh. The Jeep was gone. Mumbling something to himself about needing coffee, he telephoned his mother and headed toward the kitchen. Thirty minutes after he awoke Larry picked up the phone and called the Canton Police Department's emergency dispatch.

"This is Larry Noland. They took my wife! My wife has been abducted, do you hear me? Someone called and said my father had a heart attack, and as we were leaving for the hospital a hooded gunman came out of the trees and grabbed her. The son-of-a-bitch took my wife. Hurry! You've got to find her." Larry's courtroom drama continued as the dispatcher requested his address and kept him on the phone with additional questions.

Police cruisers with throbbing lights lined both sides of the quiet street within minutes. The neighborhood was now awake and stirring, faces peering out of windows. The officers found not only Larry waiting for them, but his parents as well, fully dressed, groomed, sipping coffee and wide awake at the predawn hour.

Larry Noland, Sr. was a striking man with graying temples and a distinctive, angular face, although one would not describe him as handsome. He was an educated man, however his personality reflected the coarseness of his upbringing. He had a long-standing reputation in town for being in the right place at the right time. It was rumored that when he found himself in a difficult financial situation with various businesses, an organized crime syndicate from St. Louis offered its help. Noland, Sr. willingly accepted the help understanding the obligation. He had close political ties to prominent people throughout the state including Congressman Wise.

Katherine Noland mirrored her husband — loud, crass and demanding. She craved attention from every source and her unhealthy closeness to her only son bordered on worship. Larry was the center of her universe and she pampered him as though he were a young child. The sole decision maker in his life, Katherine Noland's involvement was the cause of many of Sheri's and Larry's arguments. Although she displayed behavior consistent with a drinking problem, no one could ever be sure. Her behavior was always erratic.

Larry took a deep breath and began to recount his story to the officers.

"The hooded man kept saying 'move and you'll die' as he waved the gun in our faces and he handed Sheri a roll of duct tape and told her to wrap my arms and legs tight. He yelled at her 'do it now or you'll never see him again'."

Larry paused, ran his sweaty hands through his thinning hair trying to compose himself.

"Sheri wrapped my arms behind me with the duct tape, then my legs. The man pushed and shoved her with the gun while she put the tape over my eyes and mouth. She was hysterical and kept begging the man not to hurt me. He shoved the gun in her back and told her to shut up or he would shoot her. I couldn't do anything." He sobbed. "I didn't want Sheri to get hurt so I just stood there and told her to do what he said. There was nothing else I could do. Do you understand? Nothing! He forced me face-down on the driveway. He pushed Sheri into my Jeep and drove away headed south over the bridge." Larry placed his hands over his face and wept like a child.

"Mr. Noland, what time did the kidnapper take your wife?" asked an officer.

"About three this morning I think but it took me awhile to free myself from the duct tape before I could get back into the house and call the police." He cleared his throat.

The officers examined the ball of duct tape consisting of torn bits and pieces stuck together that Larry had given them, and then they placed it into a sealed evidence bag. The officers continued the long, tedious job of asking questions necessary for their investigation.

A young, rookie officer noticed that Larry had no red marks or skin irritation on the areas he claimed were covered with duct tape. No hair was missing from his head or arms as one would expect from tape being ripped off a body. And if he was facedown on the driveway with tape over his eyes, how did he know what direction the kidnapper and his wife were traveling?

CHAPTER THREE

On the day my world turned strange I arrived at work late as usual, but I swore that someday I would arrive on time just to see what it felt like, knowing it was a subconscious control issue. A legal brief had to be finalized and I dreaded the day. Briefs were my least favorite task, nevertheless I sat down at my desk as I did every morning, turned on the computer and began to read over the information. As minutes turned to hours the clock continued to tick away time oblivious to the court's deadline. Anxiety and frustration mounted as I examined the voluminous exhibits to be included.

No matter how soon you began preparing a brief it was never soon enough. Legal research was a priority as were record searches and verifications, and much to my chagrin, the actual writing and editing must be done at the last possible minute. Lunch had not been included in my time line today and my stomach disapproved.

Legal text on the computer monitor blurred into a mist and I rubbed my eyes wondering if I needed reading glasses or if the monitor was malfunctioning.

A rusted, metal building positioned alongside a row of railroad tracks running beneath a trestle appeared through the mist on the monitor. Beside the building was a sizeable dirt clearing and parallel to the clearing was a dense wooded area.

"Damn, what am I seeing?" I muttered to no one. Inside the building was a pale, young woman dressed in sweats crouched in a corner, her brunette head bent in an awkward down position. Duct tape covered her mouth and her hands appeared to be constrained with nylon cord behind her. I could see tears trickle down the young woman's face as though she felt abandoned and paralyzed with fear. Holding my breath I watched with apprehension as the picture before me became clearer. She sank further into the corner of the building as though trying to hide from whoever had placed her there. The tiny hairs on the nape of my neck began to rise and my spirit felt dark as it often did when I experienced visions.

The scene vaporized as fast as it had formed and the legal brief was back on the monitor. I stared at the words oblivious to my surroundings for several minutes. Needing to get out of my office and regain perspective before a panic attack set in or another vision appeared on the monitor, I wandered the hallway taking air into my lungs and letting it linger before exhaling, trying to relax. I could not lose the inherent fear attached to this vision and it angered me that my precious time had been invaded.

I pulled my shoulder-length hair back into a ponytail not caring how it looked, removed the shoes that had begun to hurt my feet and paced, weary of always seeing and hearing things to which only I seemed susceptible. These visions were an inherited gift from my grandmother that more often than not I perceived as a curse.

As a child, not knowing whether things were real or imagined was bewildering — not understanding that what I experienced were clairvoyant visions. As I grew older this mysterious gift intrigued rather than frightened, however the visions remained troubling. They clouded my thoughts and invaded my mind far too often.

The visions seemed to occur when I was under extreme stress or working on a critical deadline, and I often wondered if the stress facilitated the visions or if it was the other way around. Concentration was problematic because the visions interfered like watching several television shows at the same time, and rational thoughts became elusive during these times.

I'm a litigation paralegal in one of the most prestigious law firms in Atlanta, now our new home. Surf and sand along with the seagull's sad cries have been added to my list of memories. My family left all that behind six weeks ago to begin yet another journey in a new city.

I've been told that one's first impression of me is that I'm an eccentric, vivacious person with a zest for life. My family sees me as an extraordinary person only because they're somewhat biased. I'm the youngest of six and spoiled. Their opinion of me makes me laugh. They tease me about being an enigma, possessing a strange gift that limits me in many ways. They justify my odd behavior by saying I am bewitched — I was born at midnight.

Others who don't know me well have difficulty describing or understanding me. They're never quite sure how to talk to me and I think somehow I make them feel uncomfortable with my free spirit attitude one day then aloofness another. I have many acquaintances but few real friends. For most people it takes too much effort to know me. I cannot tell them that my indifference at times is the result of the emotional upheaval created by the visions.

Walking through the halls of the firm trying to understand the vision that had interrupted my work, I paused in mid-thought as Mr. Ollie McBride, senior partner of England, Nollig, McBride & Selten, P.C., passed me.

"Lynn - Lynn Conley, how's our newest paralegal? Working hard on that brief I understand. Finished it yet?" Mr. McBride's voice was soft, inquisitive.

"No sir, but I am close. Just taking a break. How are you?"

"Doing well considering my age. You know Lynn, we're happy to have you at the firm. You're just as cute as a button and such a little thing. You need to eat more."

Mr. McBride was responsible for monitoring the firm's work assigned to non-professional status employees. He was one of the oldest semi-retired senior partners but his opinion was respected, and I was not at all offended by his personal comments. Even at his age he never missed even the most insignificant details concerning the firm's employees.

Frowning he asked. "Are you all right, Lynn? You look a little pale. Are we working you too hard?"

"I'm fine, Mr. McBride. Just tired from working on the brief. Thanks for asking though," I said hoping that he didn't think something was wrong.

"What made you decide to work in the legal field if you don't mind my being so inquisitive? It's always my favorite question to ask a new employee." I smiled at his attempt to conceal his curiosity.

"Fairness has always been important to me, Mr. McBride. Someone once told me that justice was the reason we have law, and law is man's feeble attempt to teach decency to others. Lawsuits reveal how unbalanced life can be and I've always thought that somehow the law played a role in correcting that balance. I guess because I feel so strongly about justice, I seem to fit well in this environment. Besides," I said with a playful grin, "we have such interesting clients."

He smiled at my response without comment, scratched his head and scurried away not quite understanding my dry sense of humor yet impressed with the depth of my commitment. I continued down the hallway and into the library. I loved the scent of the dusty, old books. Many of the senior partners had placed their ancient leather bound editions in a special corner of the library and that space felt comforting. Often during the rush of the days I went there to find solitude. It was comforting this day.

* * * *

It was mid-September and the hot, humid Georgia air was stifling. My husband and I sat on the veranda overlooking the wooded hills surrounding our new home. We both loved the woods and the fragrance of the waning summer night, a pleasant contrast to the Florida flatlands. A whippoorwill's forlorn notes instilled a sense of peace in us and we both knew we had made the right decision moving to the suburbs of Atlanta. "Jon, I know we agonized over the decision to move here, but aren't you happy now that we did? It's beautiful."

He nodded. "Yes, I'm glad and it's a great city. Guess it was time for another change," Jon replied with a laugh. "Didn't want you to get bored staying too long in one place."

I gazed with affection at the man I loved. Jon had grown more handsome with the years, his dark hair had grayed in the temples and thinned, but his face had developed real character. His hazel eyes sparkled and the tiny lines around them seemed to smile even when he didn't. His shoulders and chest were broad, masculine, conveying incredible strength, yet his face presented a childlike gentleness.

There is always an element of adventure attached to change and neither of us was a stranger to these ups and downs. Jon and I were married 25 years ago and throughout most of the years our marriage had seemed like an adventure. Jon was employed with a Fortune 500 company and we often moved due to company transfers. Even though we had known Florida would be short-lived like most of the other states, we were not ready to move quite so soon.

Jon tried to share an amusing story about the day, his laughter filling the air. I laughed with him but wasn't listening. He continued with his story as the words faded into the night air. The memory of the young woman in the vision haunted me. I wanted to tell Jon what had happened, but I did not feel clear enough about it yet. After all it might not be anything and the continuation of a vision may not happen again for months, if ever. Without control of these visions I felt at odds with myself. They came and went as they pleased without consideration of me. I had accepted the visions as a part of my life, but I had never learned to interact with them well.

Jon's words became audible again and I tried to concentrate on his story. Reaching over I took his hand in mine needing to feel his strength and touching him brought me back to the security of reality.

* * * *

The temperature was gradually cooling as September progressed and autumn scented the air. A week had passed since the vision of the young woman, and nothing out of the ordinary had occurred since. Sometimes I am allowed to grasp a moment in a vision and then it vanishes. Unless the vision continues I do not give it a second thought. This one is different. I feel this one. Rarely are there feelings or emotions attached to visions unless you are familiar with the people in them.

Preparing for another case for trial at the firm, I worked well into the day concentrating on nothing else when again reality was veiled and the vision returned.

The young woman was once again in the small building with her hands bound, her mouth gagged. I could see only the side of her face now. Her head was down and turned against the wall of the building.

"She looks so hopeless," I whispered to myself. Feelings of desperation emanated from the woman in the vision and the same feelings began to consume me causing a cold shiver up my spine. I now see a steep, grassy hill to the left of the railroad tracks. To the right of the tracks past the building, is a deep valley. Once again as in the first vision, I see the wooded area, the clearing of dirt, the rusted, metal building and the railroad trestle.

"This vision is powerful. God, what do you expect me to do?" I realized that I had spoken out loud and looked about to see if anyone heard me. The vision vaporized.

I took a notepad from my desk drawer and began drawing what I had seen. Every detail is important in fitting together the pieces of a puzzle, and likewise the pieces of a vision. I sketched the railroad tracks as they cut their way under the trestle through the knoll, then the dirt clearing beside the woods. As a final point, I drew the metal building beside the railroad tracks that appeared to hold the young woman captive as she sat bound and gagged in hopeless desperation. A different kind of fear began to envelope me as I sketched the picture, a sense of knowing or kinship with this woman. She seemed familiar. Thinking about the people whom I had met since moving to Atlanta did not reveal any recognition. Who was she? Why was I seeing her?

* * * *

Friday evening, September 24th, one week later as I watched the news on a local television station, the face of a young woman appeared while the reporter described her abduction and pleaded with the kidnappers to return her unharmed. I knew that I had seen that face before, the pretty brunette with intelligent, sparkling eyes.

It began in the pit of my stomach, that vile, insidious feeling and worked its way up to my throat. Covering my mouth with my hand, I ran to the bathroom, tears streaming down my cheeks.

"God, help her!" I threw up.

CHAPTER FOUR

Larry's throbbing head caused unbearable pain behind his eyes making him scowl. He dreaded making this call, but having no choice, he picked up the phone, took a deep breath and punched in the numbers. Sheri's parents lived in Madison, Tennessee two hundred and fifty miles from Canton and Larry was grateful at this moment because he could not have told them face to face. The phone rang three, four times — Larry prayed that they were not home.

"Hello."

"Mr. Hilliard, it's Larry. I don't know how to tell you," he paused. "Bad news." He inhaled sharply. "I'm sorry. Sheri was kidnapped about thirty minutes ago."

"What did you say? How?" Wayne Hilliard's voice cracked.

Larry repeated the horrible events of the abduction to his father-in-law pausing several times to clear his throat. He swallowed so hard his Adam's apple tightened his throat causing him to choke. "The police are here. They'll do everything they can to find her, sir."

"We're on our way. You have my cell number. If you hear anything before we get there, call me. We'll be there as soon as possible. Are you all right?"

"Yes, sir. I'm okay considering. I'll see you soon."

Larry's father called the congressman, who in turn called the partners at Larry's firm. Police officers were swarming the Noland house by seven. The FBI was called a few hours later and family members, close friends and Congressman Wise arrived to offer support.

Embellished with a mixture of dark antiques and modern furnishing that gave it a warm, cozy feeling, the large den overflowed with activity, and it was there that Katherine Noland's high-pitched voice reverberated.

"Those people only took Sheri trying to get to my poor Larry. That's why this happened. They didn't take her for any ransom — they're trying to hurt my little boy."

"Mom, please. No one has asked for a ransom yet." Larry glared at his mother willing her to be quiet.

She clutched her son's arm as if to make sure everyone in the room knew he belonged to her while she tongue lashed the officers who tried to continue questioning Larry in spite of her clamor. The elder Mr. Noland and the Congressman slipped away to the quiet, elegant living room to discuss arrangements for a ransom should one be demanded. They both knew it would require only one phone call to the local bank president to raise the money.

The usual three-hour drive from their home in Tennessee had taken only two, and Wayne and Sarah Hilliard arrived shaken and red-eyed. Sitting on the overstuffed sofa in the den they held each other's hands as they listened to their son-in-law describe Sheri's abduction in detail.

Sarah, a strong, refined woman who maintained her outward composure even in a crisis, sat with dignity and control as she voiced her concern and fear for her daughter's state of mind and physical condition. Tears flowed down her cheeks, but her voice never quivered, and although just loud enough to be heard above Katherine Noland's screeching, her words brought an eerie stillness to the room. Wayne held her clenched hand.

"Wasn't there something you could have done to prevent this, Larry?" she asked trying to control her anger.

"No! He had a gun and I didn't want Sheri to get hurt. I thought if I cooperated with him he wouldn't hurt her," Larry said indignantly. He paced the floor, his mother never far from his side. He had never liked Sarah Hilliard very much and he just about hated her at this moment. She made him feel small and insignificant.

There was a coldness about her even though she was polite when she didn't approve of something or someone.

"How big was this man?" probed Sheri's father.

"About five-eleven probably weighing 170 pounds," said Larry, turning away from Mr. Hilliard. The investigating officers had asked him hundreds of questions over and over, and he was growing quite tired of them. He knew Sheri's father looked at him with disgust as he asked questions and Larry couldn't bear to meet his eyes. Mr. Hilliard silently blamed him.

Hilliard was a logical thinking, successful businessman, endowed with kindness, determination, and commendable moral standards, and he had raised his daughters with those traits. He adored his wife, was not ashamed for anyone to know it, and expected his daughters to receive the same devotion from their husbands after they married. He would have taken whatever measures were necessary to stop anyone who tried to hurt his family. It was inconceivable to him that the man married to his oldest daughter would not protect her.

After obtaining all the currently known facts from Larry and the police officers, Wayne and Sarah called their younger daughter, Beth who was away at the university.

Sarah chose her words with care not wanting to frighten her younger child. "Beth, sweetheart listen to me carefully. Sheri's been kidnapped. The FBI thinks it was for ransom so whoever took her probably won't hurt her."

"God! Mom? Who would do such a horrible thing? How could this happen? Why would anyone want to kidnap Sheri?" She cried out without taking a breath.

"Your father and I are at Sheri's house. The police and the FBI are here. We don't know who did this, but the FBI think they'll call soon with a ransom demand."

"I'm coming up there right now."

"Honey, please wait a little while. We don't want you driving while you're upset. It would be better if you waited until we know more about the situation," Sarah pleaded.

"Mom, I'm okay. I'm leaving right now. I'll be there in a couple of hours. I love you. Don't worry about me, all right?"

Beth tossed random clothes into a bag, raced to her car and was halfway to Canton before her mother's words sank in. Unable to see through the flood of tears, she pulled off the highway and stopped the car. Gripping the steering wheel she screamed, "Why? Why? Not my sister. Not Sheri." An hour later, weary and frightened, she hugged both her parents and held them, afraid to let go.

The vigil continued as everyone waited to hear from the kidnapper. What did he want? Where had he taken Sheri? Why had this happened? There were so many questions — and no one had answers. The local police officers were outside the house searching the area for evidence while the FBI remained inside awaiting instructions from their superior.

"Most of the time in these kinds of cases the kidnapper only wants money. We're sure to hear from him soon," Special Agent Arthur, the FBI agent in charge tried to assure the family. He then continued to bellow orders to the other officials present.

"We need recorders set up on all the phone lines here," he said as he pointed to the dining room table. "We need to be ready when this bastard calls."

"Sorry, ma'am," he acknowledged Mrs. Hilliard.

"How many phone lines do you have in the house, Mr. Noland? I don't want any surprises. People, be ready."

As the orders continued, the flow of suits and uniforms throughout the house was ominous. Special Agent Arthur was not only impressed by the power his job afforded, his ego surged at the slightest reference to his title — FBI Special Agent in Charge. He was a gaunt man, a little on the balding side, and he demonstrated definite signs of a Napoleon complex. He enjoyed watching the agents jump at his commands. However competent he thought himself to be, his instructions were always misconstrued. No one seemed to be in charge when Special Agent Arthur thought he was.

Arthur, an only child raised by old parents, was expected to act like a grown up. His father had no patience with him and when he did not measure up to the expectations, his father told him he was stupid, that he would never amount to anything in life. Arthur became a bully, passing his frustrations along to anyone smaller or younger than he. Through the years he became an expert at giving orders. Vowing that he would show his father he was not stupid, he pursued his ambition to secure a job that would give him power, one that would allow him to treat others as he had been treated, and he became the mirror image of his father.

FBI agents continued to question Larry Noland throughout the day in the hopes that he had forgotten some small detail that would either help them, or deceive him into revealing something incriminating. They reviewed the initial report provided by the officers who arrived first on the scene finding nothing suspicious. There was however, a small notation in reference to a neighbor who mentioned that while taking a walk, he saw a woman sitting in a Jeep with a scarf over her eyes. He thought it was around ten-thirty last night, but he could not remember which street he was on at the time.

FBI agents swarmed the den and dining room, placing recording equipment on the table, running electrical wires across the floor, testing the equipment and shouting to each other as they worked. Police officers took turns coming into the house to share information with the agents and the activity increased.

Above all the noise, Katherine Noland's shrill crescendos could not be ignored. Ill at ease, family members tried to comfort each other as painful hours passed, waiting for news of Sheri. Wayne Hilliard's face reflected the pain he felt inside. He paced the floor stopping once in a while to place a comforting arm around his wife or younger daughter, or to ask questions of the investigating officers.

The elder Mr. Noland remained in the living room alone, lost in thought, annoyed that his time was being wasted here at his son's house. He could not leave; it wouldn't look right. He held his head in his hands trying to block the sound of his wife's voice. *Didn't the woman ever shut up?*

In the past he had sought comfort with Molly, a young, sensual woman he had met in a bar outside the city limits. Unlike his wife with whom he had not shared a bed in years, Molly would do anything he asked of her. She made him feel good, important in ways that mattered. How he wished he were with her now instead of here being expected to play the concerned father-in-law.

He never cared for Sheri and did not like anything about her family. They were "do-gooders" always acting like they thought they were better. He never understood why his son had married her in the first place, but Larry was like his mother so what could one expect? He had never been able to pound any sense into his son's head. Larry reacted to life in the worst possible way and everything was a crisis. Always held accountable for his son's actions, Mr. Noland was damn tired of making excuses for him. The others had made it quite clear that they would have no problems with Larry or else. He knew that the 'or else' meant *he* would be dealt with and these people never played games. He could not exist without their money and their power, so in exchange, he had to keep his overzealous son in line at all times, and Congressman Wise seemed to be around to make sure that he did. He loathed his family and Sheri for placing him in this awkward position. Rubbing his throbbing head, he stumbled back into the den to join family members.

"Larry, we'll do everything in our power to get Sheri back safely," intoned Congressman Wise, placing a comforting arm around Larry's shoulder. "You know we have the best available resources at our disposal."

Evening fell like a tomb door closing on the Noland's household, now filled with sadness and anticipation. No phone call came from the kidnapper. The pungent scent of coffee filled the house as it had brewed throughout the day. Serving counters and the long kitchen table were laden with fried chicken, potato salad, fried corn, chicken and dumplings, biscuits, coconut and pecan pies, and sweetened, iced tea. No one ate. Being a long-standing Southern tradition, food was brought by neighbors and church members when words were not enough to assuage the grief. Every sound was amplified with everyone in the house anxious, waiting and wondering.

When the phone rang the house silenced like a burial ground and its intruders became stone.

"Larry, answer on the third ring," demanded Special Agent Arthur. "That'll give us time to activate the recorder for a trace. Keep him on the line as long as possible. Ready?" He counted down on his fingers — three, two and pointed to the phone.

Hearts pounding, breaths held, family members rushed into the dining room from their respective places in the house, terrified to hear this phone call yet with a desperate need to know. It was seven P.M., September 21st, sixteen tormenting hours since Sheri's reported abduction. Sucking air into his lungs through clenched teeth, Larry answered on the third ring.

"That you, Noland?" asked the raspy voice which bore a regional Southern accent, enunciating and extending each syllable.

"We got your pretty wife. I want three hundred-fifty thousand cash. You got one hour to get it or we kill her." The phone line went dead but the agents heard the demand, as did everyone in the room.

"What can I do? Can you come up with that kind of cash in one hour?" asked Larry looking at his mother, who in turn gave her husband a demanding glare. "He said they would kill her if we didn't get it. You heard him."

"Don't worry, son we've already made arrangements to get whatever we need from the bank." Mr. Noland placed a call to the bank president who was awaiting instructions. Two police officers, Larry's father and the Congressman hurried to the bank, lights flashing, sirens screaming. Not much time was left.

Wayne Hilliard paced the floor in anticipation of the next phone call. If the kidnapper received the money, Sheri would be released unharmed. There was hope — they now knew she had been taken for money and not some other senseless reason, although kidnapping for ransom was a senseless act in Hilliard's opinion. How could money ever replace human life in its importance? He would give everything he possessed to have his daughter back at this moment. *Dear God bring her home safely to us.*

Sarah's eyes were fixed upon her pacing husband while she held the hand of her younger daughter sitting beside her. Sarah imagined that if she could keep them all connected, keep them together as a family, somehow their combined strength would protect Sheri and erase her own shattered thoughts.

The bank president placed the money identified by serial numbers into a plain, brown, canvas gym bag following FBI textbook standard procedure in abduction cases. Mr. Noland and the congressman traveled back to the house, rushed inside and checked the clock. They had ten minutes to spare. Congressman Wise pitched the canvas bag to Special Agent Arthur for safekeeping, who absent-mindedly handed it to his assistant and then continued to shout at the agents. Five minutes later Larry received the second call.

"Larry, you got the cash?"

"Yeah, I've got it."

"All right, Mr. Know-It-All-Lawyer go on over to Highway 140 to Alpharetta. You listening? Go to exit 92, check into that Marriott Motel and spend some of your money, you can afford those places. I'll call you there. Shouldn't take but an hour. I'll call you then on that mobile phone you got. Give me the number."

Seeing an opportunity to get out of the stifling house and away from all these people, Mr. Noland spoke up. "Special Agent Arthur

I think it's too dangerous to send my son. Let me go in his place."

"I don't think this bastard cares who delivers the money as long as he gets it," said Arthur.

"Excuse the language, ma'am," he said to Mrs. Hilliard. "All right you can go. An unmarked car will stay out of sight behind you. Don't look for it. There will be others in position along the way. Act normal and follow his instructions. Get that money delivered so we can get Sheri back unharmed. Understand?"

Mr. Noland ripped the canvas bag from the assistant agent's hand, nodded his head that he understood and reassured his son that he would get there in time, almost forgetting to take the cell phone.

He drove into the parking lot of the Marriott at the same time an unsuspecting Alpharetta police officer making his usual rounds, pulled in directly behind him. The FBI in an attempt to keep the kidnapping quiet, failed to notify the Alpharetta Police Department of the ransom drop. Thinking only about his escape from the house, Mr. Noland failed to see the police car behind him. He checked into a room and waited for the kidnapper's call.

Watching the motel from across the street, the kidnapper saw the police car, thought it was escorting Mr. Noland and was sure they had set him up. He slammed his hand on the steering wheel and cursed them.

"I'm not stupid," he hissed. "I'll show 'em. I'll make 'em wait a long time for the next call. I'll make those bastards wish they hadn't tried to trick me."

As the morning re-birthed, the FBI instructed Larry's father to return with the ransom. They could do nothing further until the kidnapper called again. Mr. Noland checked out of the motel and cursed the FBI as he opened the car door. *Stupid bastards. Why couldn't they do something right for a change? Damn it, Larry. Why do you always screw up my life? How did I raise such an idiot?* He did not want to go back to his son's house. He wanted this to be over and he did not want to hear his wife's voice ever again.

Driving with ease, Mr. Noland returned to a house filled with trepidation. Again the family waited in agony. Some thought Mr. Noland should have stayed at the motel and waited for the call however long it took. Leaving could make the kidnapper angry — maybe angry enough to hurt Sheri or worse. Why didn't he call?

CHAPTER FIVE

Spicer had watched the bearded man pull Sheri, drugged and unresponsive out of her husband's Jeep, while Larry Noland turned his head away. After he had heard the door close, he drove off without looking back. Sheri was dragged into an old, vacant house and thrown on the floor.

Spicer waited at the vacant house until his friend Ann Weisman picked him up at two forty-five that morning to complete the first phase of the kidnapping. She had driven him to the Noland residence as prearranged so he could dispose of Larry's Jeep. The others had guarded Sheri until he returned.

Spicer had received the phone call a few days earlier and was informed that this was an urgent matter. The caller told him that he could make some easy money and would not have to do much to earn it. He had to make sure some woman was well hidden for a few days, make a few phone calls, demand a ransom and pick up the money. He could choose one person he trusted to assist, and he had contacted his old friend, Ann Weisman. She had agreed to help without hesitation.

The caller contacted two other people to assist Spicer. One was a known killer-for-hire who enjoyed his job because it was the thrill that inspired him. Spicer wondered why they would need a hired killer in a simple kidnapping, and he thought about that for a long time. Weak since his heart surgery, he physically could not handle anything strenuous, so he justified the assistance of the two men as a simple precautionary measure.

Spicer had not known or ever met the man who contacted him, but there was talk that he was an essential part of the syndicate's cocaine trafficking operation. Illegal drugs were smuggled in from Columbia through Mexico and on to California. From there selected shipments were flown in private planes to a designated area in the mountains near Canton, recovered and distributed by a large, local trucking line. False partitions were installed in the trailers and in the fuel tanks to store the cocaine. The driver's knowledge was limited to the items listed on the shipping manifests.

These trucks could pass through the Department of Transportation weigh stations without incident because the weight of the illegal drugs had been calculated to correspond to whatever products were listed on the shipping manifests.

Spicer was honored that they had chosen him for this job — he would not let them down. The woman he was hired to kidnap had overheard something that could jeopardize the syndicate's entire operation. He would make sure she was too scared to do anything after the kidnapping and once the ransom was paid, she would be returned home a little roughed up but quiet.

"Let me have her now," Spicer said upon returning with the Jeep. "I'll meet Ann and we'll complete this little deal. This is the easiest money I've made in a long time," he said.

Spicer was a weak man, middle-aged with failing health, his body uncooperative with his plans for life. After heart surgery a few weeks earlier, he tired quickly and was unable to work. He had earned a fortune in mineral exploration, but through mismanagement of his business he had lost everything. In debt beyond recovery, the medical bills had further devastated him. He would do about anything to earn money.

"Let's go, honey," he said to Sheri. "This'll be over soon. Just as quick as your husband drops off the ransom we're demanding, we'll let you go." Eyes covered and hands bound behind her, Sheri stumbled still dazed from the drugs.

Spicer drove Larry Noland's Jeep to Ann Weisman's house in a modest subdivision across the street from a dirt clearing, a rusted metal building, railroad tracks and woods where she waited impatiently.

"What took you so long?" she wailed. "Hurry up and get this over with. I don't like this one bit. You better not get caught or screw this up. Understand? You ain't paying me enough to risk getting caught."

"I'll call you in a couple of hours. You know what to do," Spicer said as he drove away.

Ann took Sheri by her bound arms and led her into the house. She pushed her into a small, dark storage room at the back of the house where she would remain. Sheri slumped in the corner of the room as tears streamed down her face. She could not see the room but her feet could touch the walls from all angles. Her shoulders ached from the strain of her bound arms behind her back. She could not control the tears and her breath struggled to escape the tape covering her mouth.

Ann and Spicer thought that it was safer to move Sheri around rather than keep her in one place, at least until the ransom was paid. Three hours later just before dawn Ann received the call she had waited for. She took Sheri deep into the national forest only a short distance from her house, and tied her to a tree. Ann was at home in these woods having grown up playing in them, and she knew every square inch. If Sheri managed to get loose she would not go very far.

"I'll take the tape off your mouth if you promise not to make any noise. Okay?" Sheri nodded and Ann pulled off the tape in one quick motion trying not to take skin with it.

"Thank you, Sheri gasped." Her swollen tongue and raw throat made it difficult to speak. She looked around but her eyes would not focus well. After a few minutes she realized that as far as she could see there were only woods, dense and foreboding, and she had no idea where she was. She tried to remember what had happened to her, but it was unclear. She recalled leaving in the Jeep with Larry to go see a surprise, and later waking up in a vacant building hearing voices she didn't recognize.

How did I get here and where is Larry? What happened to him? Who is this woman? Memory began to emerge as Sheri took deep breaths trying to still the confusion in her mind.

"What happened to my husband? Did they hurt him? That man who brought me to you said something about a ransom being paid. What was he talking about?"

Ann Weisman, a large, round woman with masculine features had short, cropped hair tinged a dull gray which gave her a rough, hard look, and her ruddy complexion indicated years of exposure to the elements.

"I don't know, honey. My job is to make sure you don't go anywhere until they come for you. I'm just doing what I'm told so don't ask questions," Ann said as she snubbed out a cigarette and lit another. "He'll come for you if everything goes okay and your old man does just like he's told. Let's make the best of this now. Tell me about your family. You have a sister, don't you? And your daddy, he's a big shot right? Got lots of money?"

"I won't discuss my family with you. They're really none of your business. What's my husband supposed to do?"

Ann ignored her question never taking her eyes off Sheri's face as the cigarette smoke circled around her head.

What if they don't let me go? Sheri wriggled her hands one at a time and watched Ann. *The ropes aren't that tight — I probably could get away, but I don't know where I am, and I can't see anything but woods. What if no one knows I'm missing?* She felt her heart pounding, faster, faster.

Just before mid-day the sound of the approaching Jeep bolted Sheri.

"Thank God. Larry's coming for me and they'll let me go," she whispered to herself.

"It's about time. Where have you been?" Ann asked.

Sheri watched Spicer as he got out of her husband's Jeep. He was a small person and did not appear to be threatening, but as he got closer Sheri realized his facial expression said otherwise. She shivered as he walked past her now realizing *he* was driving the Jeep. Larry had not come to rescue her.

"I've got to get some sleep and that's what I'm doing. I'm worn out from running around all night. You keep a good eye on her. You hear?" Spicer lay down on the ground and began to snore. His sleep was short lived interrupted by the continuing chest pain, and he gave up. He moved around in the woods rubbing his temples then his chest trying to decide what he should do next.

"I need to go home for a little while," Ann said. "The kid will be coming in from school and I need to get rid of him, send him to a friend's house or something, since this is taking longer than we thought. I'll bring back some food. I'm hungry and I know Sheri's got to be. Do you want something?" Ann asked Spicer. He continued to rub his chest and was throwing nitroglycerin tablets into his mouth one after another.

"You better not die on me. You hear? At least not until we finish this and I got my money," she chided.

"Real funny. Yeah, I'm hungry. Hurry up though. I got calls to make and things to do so we can finish this job."

Spicer stared through Sheri. He did not talk to her, did not look at her yet she knew somehow he was watching. She did not want to stay in the woods with this man or anyone for that matter — but he frightened her. At least the woman talked to her. He just stared with a strange look in his eyes as though she was not even there. Sheri sat on the tree stump and waited for the woman to return. She wriggled her tied hands and thought again of ways to escape. If she could get her hands free then she could untie her legs and run. She knew he could not chase her because he was sick, but he had a gun and she knew that he would use it. Besides, where would she go? There was nothing but woods and she was still too dazed to think straight. She waited, hoping the woman would soon return.

A few hours later Ann returned with sandwiches and a grimy thermos of coffee. Sheri knew she should eat, but the sight of the disgusting food and watching Ann and Daniel devour it as though they were starved made her nauseous.

Sheri asked, "Can I get up and walk around? My legs are numb and my arms hurt."

"You take her. I aim to finish eating," Daniel instructed as he shoved half of the sandwich into his mouth.

Ann untied the ropes that held Sheri's arms spread-eagled to the trees on each side of her and then untied her legs. She tried to stand but her body, stiff and sore felt strange. Her arms felt detached from the rest of her body and her legs were unsteady. She felt faint and stood very still for a few moments before attempting to move. Ann tied a length of rope around Sheri's waist and walked her like an animal on a leash. Asking permission to relieve herself was humiliating in front of this woman. There was no privacy, but she would have to endure the embarrassment.

Her mind was clearing and memory resurfacing, however what took place between the time she left with Larry and awoke in the vacant house was a mystery. She remembered something being said about her husband paying a ransom. If they were waiting for a ransom … *oh my God, it's me. They've kidnapped me.*

The shocking realization that she had been abducted gripped her mind with terror as the rope leash led her around. Larry would pay their ransom; they would let her go. At least she knew he was safe and that meant other people knew she was missing. Confusion crossing her face, she looked at Ann then at Spicer, not understanding why they would want to kidnap her. Fear once again tried to override her temporary calm. *Think about anything, anything except what could happen.* Sheri inhaled the musty air trying to slow her heartbeat knowing she must focus on something, anything visible in the woods that would help stabilize her irrational thoughts.

Forcing herself to look at Ann closely for the first time, she saw sea green eyes scowling under the brows. Their color reminded Sheri of a woman she once met long ago in her childhood, and she wondered where this woman was now, and wondered still why she had been so drawn to her. The woman had been her grandmother's new neighbor and she had come over for a visit.

Sheri was a timid child, sensitive and felt emotions way beyond her young years. Needing more physical affection than her younger sister Beth, her grandmother instinctively knew this, and even though she loved both girls she lavished Sheri with attention.

Sitting in her grandmother's sweet, cookie-smelling, cozy kitchen talking about school projects that day, she could not take her eyes off the woman. She was drawn to her like a magnet. It was her eyes, the greenest eyes she had ever seen, and they danced like flames of green fire when she laughed. It was a comforting feeling — like sharing with a best friend. She had liked her grandmother's new neighbor.

Sheri remembered darting across the room and throwing her arms around the woman, hugging her as she left her grandmother's house that day. It was as much a surprise for Sheri as it was for her grandmother's new neighbor. That gesture formed an instant, undeniable bond that neither the child nor the neighbor understood. Sheri remembered looking across the street at the empty house after the neighbor and her family had moved away, and wondered why she felt so sad, why she had missed her so much. Why was she thinking about her now thirteen years later?

Ann returned Sheri to the tree stump and once again tied her arms and legs spread-eagle to the trees. The day passed at a snail's pace as Sheri sat on the tree stump chair. Ann made small talk and napped, but she was very aware of her ward. Sheri listened to the silence of the woods. A falling acorn reminded her of Chicken Little and the sky falling, a much loved childrens' story that her mother read to her at bedtime. Leaves fluttered to the ground without echoing as they settled in for the winter. Birds, high in the trees chirped as they made nests of sticks and rotting leaves. In a fairy tale the feathered friends would have untied the princess held captive in the forest by the wicked witch. Why didn't these feathered friends help her? Sheri could only dream. This was no fairy tale. This was an awake, living nightmare.

She tried to think of anything other than her family. The tears flowed when she considered how scared and frantic her parents must be. She thought of nursery rhymes from her childhood and tried to remember their lines, books she had read, and tried to remember their authors. She tried to remember the questions on her bar exam. Nothing worked. Sheri was too scared to remember. She wanted to go home to her parents. She was a frightened, lonely, adult child who wanted her mother to hold and comfort her, her dad to speak to her and brush the hair from her forehead once again. She needed to hear their voices. Tears streamed down her cheeks and she lowered her head in anguish.

Spicer hid Larry Noland's Jeep deep in the woods on an unused logging road, and got back into his truck that he had left there the day before the kidnapping. Leaving Ann and Sheri in the woods, he drove back to his house to make an appearance so his family would not be concerned. He would need to justify his absence from home the previous night and needed an alibi. A poker game should do fine.

* * * *

Sleep eluded the Noland household. The Hilliards listened to Special Agent Arthur, trying to understand his obscure plans to rescue their daughter. Throughout the night they implored God to answer their prayers for Sheri's safe return. Larry's father telephoned several times from the motel to let them know that he had not heard from the kidnapper. Katherine Noland sipped brandy with her coffee and clutched her son's hand. Throughout the night Sarah crept through her daughter's house touching Sheri's belongings. She paused to gaze at her daughter's wedding picture remembering another time, a happier time, then continued her aimless wandering until she was back in the den with the others who waited.

"What do you think happened?" asked one of the FBI agents.

"Who knows? Maybe he changed his mind at the last minute. You never know what these creeps think. They're all psychotic," said Special Agent Arthur.

"Do you think we screwed up by sending Mr. Noland?"

"Hell no. We didn't screw up. We'll get the son-of-a-bitch," Arthur shouted and realizing he was cursing again, looked around for Mrs. Hilliard.

"Maybe he's jerking us around watching to see if we follow his instructions before he makes a move," another agent offered.

* * * *

Spicer drove back to the woods where Sheri and Ann waited, slammed the door on the truck as he stepped out, grabbed his chest and groaned. The pressure on his arms tore at the incision in his chest. He was so angry he did not realize he had slammed the door until it was too late.

"Your old man's an idiot," he yelled at Sheri. "He can't do nothing right. Couldn't even drop off the money like he was told. They'll get him for being so stupid." Spicer was not only angry — he was scared. Getting the ransom should have been easy — he had told Larry what to do. Why couldn't he just do it?

"Let's go, bitch. You'll pay for this." Enraged, Daniel shoved his gun in Sheri's face and started yelling at Ann. "Untie her and put her in the truck then you get out of here. Go straight home before someone sees you."

Ann was frightened. She had never seen Spicer so angry. She placed Sheri in the truck, fastened her seat belt, patted her on the shoulder and hurried back to her car. She drove away wondering if he would kill her.

The angrier Daniel became the faster he drove. The woods were now dark and the truck's headlights bouncing off the trees cast ghostly shadows around them. Sheri's arms were tied behind her and only the seat belt prevented her from being thrown out of the truck as it veered around curves in the road. Inside the truck the same apparitions appeared, but they were tinged in a strange green glow from the lighted dashboard. Spicer's face looked distorted in the light with greenish black holes where his eyes and mouth should have been. The gun was crammed inside his jacket pocket, its handle showing as a reminder.

"Please don't hurt me," Sheri pleaded, her voice quivering as tears streamed down her face. "I didn't do anything. Why are you so angry with me?"

"Shut up!" You don't know when to keep your mouth shut. That's why you're here, stupid bitch. You shouldn't have told anyone what you heard, especially not your idiot husband. Now he can't even follow instructions. They're going to be pissed!" Spicer yelled.

His anger was so volatile that Sheri was sure he would kill her. She opened her mouth to scream, but the sound froze in her throat, and she collapsed over the dashboard in agony. Spicer began to slow down as he saw the city lights glimmer through the darkness and he began to calm, no longer yelling at Sheri. In spite of his anger, he felt sorry for her as he realized how frightened she was.

With controlled sympathy he said, "I'll let you call your husband but you say what I tell you to say. You got that?"

Sheri nodded not daring to speak, afraid that she would anger him again. She needed to hear Larry's voice to know how and why this happened. He would tell her if he was able. She would stay very quiet and do exactly as Spicer said. He stopped at a pay phone in a remote area and after coaching Sheri he allowed her to make the call.

"Larry, baby, it's Sheri. Thank God you're all right. I didn't know what had happened to you. He said that you're to go to Michael Runyan's house. He'll call you there in one hour. He said you better have the money."

"Yeah, I understand." Larry said nothing else. Sheri prayed for him to tell her what was taking place. Why didn't he say something?

"Oh God, Larry I'm so scared. Why did they take me?" Sheri cried into the phone. Spicer grabbed it out of her hand and slammed it down onto its cradle.

"I told you not to say nothing except what I told you to say!" he shouted at her.

"Get back in the truck and lay down in the seat."

He grabbed duct tape from under the seat, torn off a piece and covered her mouth.

"Now I bet you won't say nothing else."

Daniel drove around for forty-five minutes then found another pay phone to call Michael Runyan's house. Mr. Runyan answered the phone.

"Where's Noland?"

"Sorry, he's not here yet. Can I take a message?" Spicer slammed down the phone.

"Where the hell is he?" he mumbled to himself. He waited a few more minutes and dialed the phone again. Runyan answered. Daniel's anger escalated. He called several more times and at last Larry answered.

* * * *

Darkness had closed its hand over the light when the phone rang. Special Agent Arthur was so busy giving conflicting orders and arguing with his staff, he and the technical agents had not had time to react to the sound. Larry did not wait. Agent Hobbs, a pretty, intelligent, brunette standing beside Larry watched him with an ambivalent stare while she listened with interest. She could not hear the caller's voice, but she saw the tape on the recorder whirling on its spindle, capturing the conversation.

"Yeah, I understand. I'll go to his house. Right. Now. That's right. I have the money. Yeah, I know what to do. Okay? Let's get on with this," Larry snapped at the caller and replaced the phone on its cradle. "That was Sheri."

Agent Hobbs stared at Larry, confusion covering her face like a shroud as his words sank in. Unable to control her rage she shouted, "What kind of a cold-hearted bastard are you? That was your wife who was kidnapped and you spoke to her that way? You didn't reassure her that everything possible was being done to find her? What is your problem?"

Stoic, Larry stared at the wall as though he had not heard anything the female agent asked him. She was seething.

"That's quite enough, Agent Hobbs," shouted Special Agent Arthur. "You know better. Consider yourself excused from this room. Now!" Agent Hobbs glared at Larry again. She started to protest, thought better of it and left the room. *You better be completely above reproach Larry Noland. I'm going to watch you closely on and off duty.*

"Well, what did she say?" Arthur snarled.

"I'm to take the money to Michael Runyan's house and wait for another call. He's the senior partner at my firm. I have one hour," said Larry.

Special Agent Arthur raised his eyebrows but said nothing.

His face hard, Wayne Hilliard fought to gain control of his emotions. He would never interfere with the FBI's efforts to get his daughter back, but to know she called and not be allowed to hear her voice was devastating. Thank God Sarah was in the back of the house and did not know. He studied Larry's face in stunned silence, questions churning in his mind.

"Replay the tape. I want to hear my daughter's voice to know that it was really her on the phone."

Special Agent Arthur nodded to the technician to replay it. He wanted to hear it as well. The tape whirred on its spindle in reverse, stopped and then began forward. Nothing but static. They exchanged puzzled glances and the technician tried again; only static, background noise. Not even Larry's voice had recorded.

"What the hell happened?" shouted Special Agent Arthur. "You better get this problem fixed now, not one second later but now." He was furious with the technician and with Larry. Why couldn't anyone follow instructions? Now another problem. Noland would need to be wired. *What kind of game was being played here?* Arthur felt as though he was being manipulated, but by whom he was not sure.

"We'll have to get you wired since there's no recording devices set up at Runyan's house," Arthur bellowed. "When you get the next phone call maybe we'll be able to hear that conversation if this damn thing will work. People do your job for once."

His assistant began placing the wiring device on Larry's body by the book. Congressman Wise and Larry's father insisted that they be allowed to go with him to the Runyan home. Arthur did not object but the assistant agent thought it odd that both men needed to accompany him again. After all, agents would be with him every step of the way. He stored that thought away in his mind for future reference.

Testing the wiring device took longer than anticipated, and Larry was thirty minutes late arriving at the senior partner's house. He missed the phone call. Hours later the kidnapper called Michael Runyan's house.

"Larry, you don't have a brain in your head. You screwed me around last night and I've just about had enough of this. If you want to see your wife again you do what I say. She's feeling real bad right now so you better not cross me."

"No, I haven't. I did exactly what you said," Larry argued.

"Yeah, yeah, you have. You got the police there and you got

everybody else with you. You get rid of those folks. I mean all of them. You hear me? I'll call you at your house tomorrow night at eight and you better be there and ready to leave when I say leave. Now, I want another hundred thousand cash. You didn't deliver and now you'll pay big."

"Dad, he wants another hundred thousand by tomorrow night," Larry said. "He's pissed because he didn't get the ransom last night and because I was late getting to Runyans."

Mr. Noland rubbed his forehead between his eyebrows and sighed.

"Don't worry, son. We'll get the money. I think I have that much cash in the vault at my office. If not, between Hilliard, the bank and what I have, we can work it out. You'll have it in the morning one way or another," he said. *Hilliard should be paying all the money. It's his daughter who caused this problem.*

"Larry, if I can do anything, anything at all, son, don't hesitate to ask," Michael Runyan said. "The firm will help in any way possible. Remember, we're a family here and we take care of our own."

CHAPTER SIX

Once again Sheri's family, the FBI agents and police officers settled in for a bleak night. The kidnapper appeared to be playing games and even though they did not expect another call until the following evening, they could not afford to take any chances.

Earlier in the evening Larry's mother had given him a sleeping pill knowing her boy could not handle the pressure. In her opinion, the police and FBI were brutal with their constant questioning and accusing eyes. All this waiting — it was more than he should have to endure, so she would make sure they left him alone. Sheri had no right to cause his suffering. How dare she do this to him?

Katherine Noland poured herself a brandy, kicked off her shoes and curled up on the sofa. She would keep a close eye on her son while he slept allowing no one to disturb him. She studied the Hilliards sitting side by side, shoulders touching, and she wished these intruders would leave her son's house.

"I feel helpless and I can't just sit here waiting. I'm going out to look for Sheri," Hilliard said to his wife and headed to the door.

"Wait I'll go with you," Sarah called out to him.

"No. You stay here and try to get some rest. I have to do this alone."

An agent questioned Hilliard wanting to know why he was leaving the house, but then let him go on his way and sent a police officer to accompany him. Sarah had looked into her husband's tormented eyes, then over at Larry who was sleeping like a baby on the sofa. *He should be the one out searching for Sheri. He let the kidnapper take her. God forgive me but I despise him right now. How could he just lie there and sleep as though he hadn't a care in the world?*

53

He should have gone with Wayne to search for his wife, my daughter, my baby.

As she continued to glare at Larry her rage escalated, and when she could stand no more, she fled outside to the patio. Never in her entire life had she felt anger of this intensity toward another human being, and she was ashamed for succumbing to its power.

Hilliard drove down black, abandoned streets stopping to search for his daughter at every run-down, vacant house he passed, sure that she was being held captive in one of them. His thoughts tormented him. He *needed* to hate Larry for allowing this man to take Sheri, but he could not. If he hated Larry then it was a reflection of how he felt about himself. He had given his daughter to Larry, entrusted her life to him when he had escorted her down the church aisle two years ago. Did that make him a failure as Sheri's father? What did that say about his judgment? Hilliard knew he had to find his daughter or he would slide into a dark, horrible place. Because he was not a self-destructive man, he knew these thoughts were counter productive. *Concentrate on Sheri — not Larry. Find her.*

Driving down a deserted, dark alley he searched for any sign of Larry's Jeep. Trying to rid his head of the pounding, confusing thoughts; he rubbed his forehead and squinted. Hilliard knew the Jeep was hidden somewhere in this town. *Think, think. What would I have done were I in the kidnapper's shoes?*

He braked the car to a halt, jumped out and ran into an old, abandoned warehouse just as his flashlight flickered. The officer drew his pistol and followed Hilliard.

"Damn light," he muttered, shaking it until it came back on. Hilliard stood in the middle of the building shining the light up at the rafters, then down over the dirt floor finding nothing but an empty building. Vacant houses and buildings stood in shambles in the town since no one cared enough to repair them or tear them down.

Continuing down another dark side street, Hilliard caught a glimpse of a chrome bumper shining in the dim light behind another abandoned house. He slammed on the brakes and jumped out of the car before it stopped completely causing the officer's head to hit the windshield. It was an older model Jeep and not even the right color. He leaned against its hood gasping for breath thinking he was going to throw up, but with determination he went through the back door of the old house not waiting for the officer. He had to know.

Broken furniture, water-soaked mattresses and filth filled the house, along with a snoring man lying on the muddy floor, his crack pipe beside him. Rats scurried through the old house.

With slumped shoulders and a heavy, hurting heart Hilliard forced himself back to the car. He leaned his head against the top of it, and for the first time since learning of his daughter's abduction, he wept openly without pride, not caring that the officer heard him. Not knowing what to do, the officer just stood beside Wayne, surprised at his own level of emotion while tears slid down his cheeks onto his stiffly starched shirt collar. Embarrassed by his lack of control, he stared at the ground hoping Hilliard would not notice.

Both of them, drained and numb, returned to Sheri's house too spent to continue searching. Hilliard could share his thoughts with no one, not even his beloved wife. This was his burden to bear alone.

* * * *

Arriving at the vacant house once again, Sheri was handed over to the others. A man with long, dark hair and a beard grabbed her by her bound arms and threw her onto the floor. With terror-filled eyes Sheri stared at the man. Dead, hollow eyes stared back. "He's trying to screw us!" Spicer said. "I'm giving him 'til tomorrow morning and then we're getting our money. I've got to get some sleep. Damn this surgery anyhow; my chest hurts. Keep an eye on her." Spicer stretched out on the floor in a corner of the house and was asleep within minutes.

Afraid to move Sheri looked around the dark room. The vulgar and repulsive bearded man who grabbed her was talking to a large sandy-haired man and a young woman. Sheri could hear only their voices, but not their words over Spicer's snoring.

The bearded man was nasty and rancid. His long hair was stringy and unkempt, and his beard and mustache needed a trim. Enormous gold chains hung around his neck and one had a grotesque carved serpent pendant attached. He watched Sheri with cold, dead eyes never taking them off her. Each time she glanced at him he licked his lips or made some obscene gesture with his hands. She shivered and looked down at the floor.

She was hungry but knew she could not eat; she needed water but none was offered. Exhausted, Sheri fell asleep on the floor where she was thrown.

* * * *

Spicer woke at seven o'clock the following morning ready to get on with his plans. He tried to get up off the floor but his body was stiff and his limbs moved with difficulty. His sleep had not been restful because his chest continued to hurt, and he remembered having a nightmare. The police were chasing him and firing their pistols, and even though he ran as fast as his legs would allow, they were closing in. Any minute he knew one of their bullets would find him. He awoke knowing the nightmare was an omen because getting the ransom was taking too long. Every second wasted made it easier for the police to find him. He was not waiting until night to make that call. He had to finish this now. Spicer tried again to get up, stretched then maneuvered around the room holding onto the walls and over to the window. It was quiet.

"Keep her here while I go get the money," he said. "This will take awhile so meet me at the other place around eight tomorrow morning. You know where I'm talking about so don't be late, and you better not do anything to her either. She's got to make another call and I don't want her to have a breakdown before she does that. Understand? After I've got the ransom and she's made the call, we take her back to the woods and let her go. You just make sure she's in one piece when you bring her tomorrow morning."

Spicer was hungry and wanted a good breakfast and he needed time to collect his thoughts before he started making phone calls again. He looked at Sheri lying on the floor and thought about his own daughters.

* * * *

Around ten o'clock the following morning the call came, a surprise the agents were not expecting. Larry looking refreshed from his drug induced, restful slumber answered the phone on the third ring.

"You got my money?"

"Yeah, I've got it."

"Okay, all right now. You know where the 7-11 is on 35th Street across them railroad tracks? The one in Alpharetta? Go there and I'll call you, and hurry. You hear? You got one more stop to make after that. Now if there's a problem and I don't show back up to get your wife they'll kill her. Understand? I'll let her call you after the last stop." He hung up.

Larry grabbed the canvas bag containing the ransom including the additional hundred thousand dollars. Special Agent Arthur gave detailed instructions this time prepared for the ransom drop. Following routine FBI procedures, they placed a tracking pager into the bag with the ransom. Larry was given an identical pager and instructed to place it on his belt. He was also wired so the FBI could listen to the phone calls.

"Both pagers are programmed to the same frequency, Larry," Special Agent Arthur said. "The Congressman has been kind enough to arrange the use of several private planes, and we'll have them in the air monitoring the frequency. Once you get the drop instructions we'll follow the signal and know exactly where you are at all times. After you place the bag at the drop site, turn off the pager on your belt. The planes will follow the tracking signal coming from the bag in the kidnapper's possession, and we'll find your wife within a short time. Understand?"

"Yes sir, I understand. I'll turn off my pager when I drop the money. Now let me get out of here so I don't miss that phone call."

Numerous agents assisted by local police officers and the Congressman's pilots listened to the constant ping of the pager signals.

Larry drove to the 7-11 as instructed and waited by the phone booth. Hours passed before the phone finally rang. He was instructed to go to a second phone booth in a different part of the city, and then continuing to drive to each location as he was instructed, he would wait for the next phone call. While he waited his mind wandered. He didn't want to think about Sheri, didn't want to know if they were hurting her. Sometimes he reasoned, a person just had no choice — some things were not controllable.

Larry knew the end of this nightmare would come at some point, and his life would once again return to normal, even better than normal. He had proven his loyalty and in return he would lack for nothing. This was a small price to pay considering the alternative they had given him. After all, Sheri had not made any significant contribution to the world yet and he had. Already secure in a position of power, it could only improve.

Not ready to give up his life for anyone, he would continue to tell himself that he had no choice. They had made it quite clear to him what would happen if he did not follow their requests. Why did Sheri have to be such an honorable person? He had known what she would do with the information she had overheard and it was his duty to inform them. Why couldn't she mind her own business? The ringing phone brought him back to full attention.

"Larry go to the parking lot at the drugstore on 55th Street. You know the one across town. Park in the lot and walk to the phone booth. Put my deposit in the booth and then leave. You better not screw up this time or she's dead."

* * * *

Spicer watched as Larry drove into the parking lot. His nerves were on edge and every sound made him flinch. He had never kidnapped anyone before and did not think he ever would again. It was too stressful considering his ill health. Perhaps a few years ago he could have handled it with skill but not now. He wanted it to be over.

Larry again followed the instructions. He got out of his car and started toward the phone booth when a slightly built hooded man, touched him on the arm startling him. He had not even heard the man approaching.

"I'll take this now. You've done your job. Get back in your car and get the hell out of here."

Larry handed over the canvas bag containing the ransom and the pager, and sprinted back to his car not looking back. He recognized the man's voice as the voice on the phone, but he had not seen a face. Larry turned his head slightly in the direction of the hooded man as he opened the car door, just in time to see the man's body sag. The hooded man grasped his chest then disappeared into the blackness beside the drugstore. Before getting back into his car, Larry searched the area for any sign of other people, but there was no one in the parking lot. Behind the drugstore was a six-foot wire fence, but he did not see a gate or any access to the street behind. The man appeared to be in pain and not physically fit enough to scale the fence and Larry wondered where he had gone. The man had vanished into the dark without a sound.

As he drove out of the parking lot Larry noticed that no cars were visible on the street, including the FBI and local police officers that were supposed to be following him. Considering that it was two morning, he thought they would have to be dis-

is rear-view mirror toward the side of the drug-

a dark colored pickup on the street behind the

but he still did not understand how the man got over the fence.

Larry began the hour drive back to his house dreading the questions he would be asked. He felt sick and wanted this to be over. Thoughts of Sheri could not be allowed in his mind, not even for a brief moment. Larry realized that he was more afraid than ever yet he had done what was demanded of him, and he could not understand the reason for his fear. The agents following Larry not only lost sight of him several times, but his pager must have malfunctioned because they were unable to track him at times. When they arrived at the drop site Larry was gone, but the telephone booth was in full view even though the streetlight was dim. The agents parked and waited, watching for any sign of the kidnapper.

Two male agents had been assigned the duty of following Larry. Special Agent Arthur thought men always executed an assignment better than women because, in his opinion, men were more aggressive. "They've got more guts," he would say.

"We'll get this one. He doesn't have a chance in hell of picking up that ransom unnoticed," the agent proclaimed to his partner.

"Why do you think he picked this place?"

"Who knows why these people do anything? Perhaps this is close to where he's keeping Sheri, if she's even alive."

"The husband, there's something not right about his story. He keeps changing from 'he took her' to 'they took her,' and he acts like he's hiding something. He's a strange one anyway. Was there one kidnapper or more than one?"

"Who knows? People get real shaken up under pressure and they don't always say the same thing each time they're questioned. Besides, all lawyers are odd. Why should he be different?"

The agents drank coffee to stay alert and continued to watch the phone booth. They discussed their varying opinions about lawyers, the special agent in charge and justice in the world. An hour later when no one had retrieved the canvas bag, they got out of the car with pistols drawn, and approached the phone booth. It was empty. They had not seen anyone, but when they arrived on the site they did not investigate. They assumed the ransom was there.

"Get Special Agent Arthur on the radio. How the hell did this happen? We'll lose our jobs over this."

As the agent explained the situation to Arthur, he offered one excuse after another knowing that his superior would be furious. Instead, Special Agent Arthur barked in his usual tone, "That's okay. The planes will have tracked the signal by now and we will know soon where Sheri is. No harm done this time."

"Special Agent Arthur we have a positive I.D. on the location of the kidnapper based on the signal transmitted by the pager," blurted the voice over the radio.

"Great! Give me the coordinates."

As Arthur checked his map he yelled, "What the hell are you people doing? That's the Noland residence."

Larry arriving home found Special Agent Arthur red-faced pacing the floor.

"Larry, you turned off your pager when you dropped the ransom so the planes could pick up the other signal, didn't you?"

Pausing to take a deep breath, Larry checked the pager attached to his belt.

"Sorry, guess I was so nervous that I forgot to turn it off."

* * * *

In the pink flush of dawn the bearded man placed Sheri in the trunk of a white Lincoln town car and drove her to meet Spicer in the next county, fifty miles away. She was weary. They had left her on the floor of the vacant house the previous day allowing her to get up to use the filthy, abandoned toilet when she could wait no longer. She was allowed to eat one dry, stale sandwich during the day, and had only a few drops of water. Her parched throat ached and her swollen tongue filled her mouth. Tape over her mouth left in place for hours had chapped and torn her lips. Her bound arms pulled together behind her caused excruciating pain in her shoulders. No one cared.

Her sole reprieve from the dead eyes and the crude words of the bearded man came when he took occasional walks outside the house, but even then he was within listening distance. While he was inside the house he tormented her.

"Hey, baby. I know jest what ya need," he taunted. "That perty little ole mouth oughta be kissed 'stead of taped." He leaned over her, stuck out his tongue and licked her face. His breath was foul and the odor lingered. Sheri cringed.

He grabbed her breasts and buried his face in them grinding his body against hers. Sheri kicked at him but he held her down on the floor. She could not scream or get away and her eyes were wild with panic. The bearded man laughed and then jumped off of her.

"You're turning me on, bitch," he said swinging around to wink at the sandy-haired man. He dropped his pants as he laughed, displayed his erection and pushed it in her face. A muffled scream mingled with his laughter. Sheri shivered and looked away unable to bear the thought of his words becoming reality.

* * * *

Arriving at the designated area, they met Spicer as planned. With the ransom finally in hand, he was tired and wanted to go home but they had a few things left to do. Making sure no one was watching, Sheri was taken out of the town car's trunk and placed in Spicer's truck. She was relieved to be back in his care. At least he was somewhat decent to her. Spicer drove to an old gas station in a secluded area just over the county line a short distance, stopped and had Sheri make her final phone call. He would let her talk as long as necessary knowing that the FBI would trace her call to that county. That would confuse the agents for a time.

"Larry, it's Sheri. The man said I could call you and just talk this time. He has the ransom and he said they would let me go soon. I'm so scared." Sheri's voice trembled as she tried to sound calm. "How much longer will they hold me?" She tried not to cry. She knew it angered Larry and the last thing she wanted was for him to be angry with her.

"It's okay. He has the money and now you're safe. Just do what he tells you to do. You'll be home very soon. I promise you," Larry said.

"Are Mom and Dad there with you? Can I talk to Daddy? I want to go home." Sheri sobbed into the phone.

"It's all right, Sheri. Your parents are okay. They aren't here right now though. You'll be home soon. Just stay calm, baby."

"If anything happens to me, Larry, I want you to know that I love you. Whatever happens please know that. I don't know why they kidnapped me and it doesn't even matter now, I just want all this to be over. You gave them the money so they have no reason to keep me now. Do they?" She was sobbing so hard that Spicer snatched the phone out of her hand and hung it up. He placed his arm around her and helped her back to his truck.

Spicer wondered if she would have a breakdown before they could complete this ordeal. He had never seen anyone so scared. He could not place the tape back over her eyes with her crying like that. So what if she saw anything now? She knew what everyone looked like anyway and Spicer knew she would never dare describe them to the police once they let her go. They had put the fear of death in her and she would keep her mouth shut forever. He was convinced of that because he had done his job well.

He proceeded north driving on desolate back roads. County road 249 was isolated and eliminated considerable time. He had been instructed to take Sheri to the old mine and swap vehicles before continuing on to the woods. He did not want any surprises now that he had the money.

As far as one could see there was just space, sheltered by rocks that were stacked perilously like building blocks teetering over the road. A waterfall played a haunting tune in the cavernous rocks at the end of the dirt road. Spicer had been instructed to drive the white town car back to the city and leave it in a parking lot to be retrieved in a few days. The bearded man would take Sheri back to the woods and let her go unharmed. The money would be distributed among the others a few weeks later, but until then, Spicer would hide it.

The bearded man drove Spicer's dark pickup truck out of the mine onto county road 249 and headed north. Sheri watched closely for anything that would distinguish the area, but it was completely desolate. There were woods on both sides of the road and virtually no traffic except for an occasional logging truck. She noticed timber sites along the way and large concrete tiles on each side of the road. She saw a rusted road sign with a missing middle number followed immediately by an old, abandoned farmhouse. As she watched, she felt the cold hand of death on her spine and she began to recite the Lord's Prayer — "Our Father, Who art in Heaven ..."

"Shut up, bitch."

Sheri felt a sharp pain across the left side of her head and then the abyss beckoned.

CHAPTER SEVEN

Over the weekend I listened to endless media broadcasts. Every television station, radio station and newspaper within a 200-mile radius reported the kidnapping of Sheri Noland. Her picture was shown in the hopes that someone somewhere had seen her and would call the FBI.

A legal assistant at my law firm lived in the same area where Sheri Noland was abducted. I arrived at the firm before work Monday morning to allow time to talk to her before beginning my day, hoping she might help me sort out the details of the area I had seen in my vision. I walked upstairs to her office, knocked on the door and walked in feeling very uncomfortable about discussing this with her.

Sheila sat at her desk drinking coffee trying to wake up. She wore her long, dark, auburn hair swept back revealing prominent cheekbones that emphasized her large, dark blue eyes. Her coloring contrast was beautiful.

"Morning, Sheila. I've got a quick question if you don't mind," I said trying to be cheerful.

"Hi, Lynn. What's up?"

"You live in Canton. Don't you?" I inquired trying to be casual.

She nodded. "Yes, I've lived there all my life. Why?"

"If I show you a sketch of a particular area, do you think you could tell me if it might be in Canton?"

"Possibly. Let's see."

Sheila took the sketch and looked at it. "I think I've been in this area before but I'm not sure. My boyfriend and I walk in the woods searching for Civil War artifacts sometimes, and this looks like one of the places we've been." She studied the sketch again and then turned her attention to me. "You look stressed out. What's this about?"

"I need any information I can find about this area. It's important but I haven't lived here long enough to know much about Atlanta or its surroundings," I said trying to avoid her question.

"Does this have something to do with one of our cases?"

I lied, "Perhaps."

"My Uncle Henry works with the railroad and would recognize this area because of the railroad tracks. I'll find out," she said and placed a call to her uncle while I waited. He asked her to bring the drawing to him that afternoon. I prayed that Sheila's uncle could identify the area. I knew the kidnapped woman had been there and maybe was there still. I also knew time was critical if she was to be rescued.

Working hard throughout the day I tried to concentrate on preparing for a trial, but Sheri Noland's face kept creeping into my mind. As she sat slumped in the corner of the building I saw tears streaming down her anguished face, and I wondered about the people responsible for her abduction. A haunting familiarity skirted around the edges of my mind again and I wanted to go home — home to the security of my family. I felt so alone at that moment and I did not know why.

Sheila called me to her office the following morning with good news. Her Uncle Henry did know the area having traveled through it many times, and he knew the exact location of the railroad tracks. I would have no choice but to tell Sheila the truth and trust her to help me. I did not want to explain the visions to her but if they revealed anything that would help locate Sheri it was worth the effort.

"Sheila, I need to explain what all this is about, but it's difficult."

"Go ahead I'm listening," she said smiling and leaned back in her chair waiting for me to begin.

"When I was a kid I was always telling my parents about things I saw and heard. They knew something was different about me because it was not possible for me to have known some of those things at my age. They worried that I might have a psychological disorder so they had several doctors run tests. To their astonishment the doctors explained that I appeared to have clairvoyant abilities. There was no physical explanation."

Sheila sat in silence with a look of complete confusion on her face. I continued. "This is difficult to explain." I shifted in my chair, crossing and uncrossing my legs.

"I've had visions since I was very young and it seems that I possess a sixth sense which allows me to see or hear things that most people cannot." Sheila sat unmoving as though spellbound, and listened without responding or asking questions. I became more uncomfortable and began to think I should not say anything further when she said, "This is fascinating. Please go on."

"I also have dreams that appear to be premonitions and I am very sensitive to other people's feelings or emotions. I can walk into a room and feel what others are feeling as I pass by them — anger, happiness, irritation. At times people tend to think I'm scatterbrained but that's not it at all. The visions cause a lot of distraction in my mind and my thoughts get muddled." I tried to laugh but the look on Sheila's face stifled it.

"I know all of this sounds preposterous and you think I'm nuts, but for you to understand why the drawing is important you have to hear it all."

She nodded, and reached for her coffee cup. I continued. "Sheila, I'm not explaining this very well at all because it's not a subject I can talk about with everyone. People have a tendency to think that I'm psychotic when they find out." I laughed but Sheila continued to study my face and sip her coffee.

"They either react out of fear or they disbelieve me. The ones who are afraid avoid me like the plague; the others gossip. I'm no different from anyone else." I smiled and shrugged. "I just have unusual abilities."

She leaned across her desk toward me as though she feared she would miss something. I waited for her to ask questions, but still she said nothing. I went on.

"My mother would always tell me that things unfamiliar or unknown frightened people because they couldn't understand and I needed to be careful. The term psychic conjures up images of spooky old women with shawls wrapped around their shoulders gazing into crystal balls. I hate that image and I would never refer to my ability as a psychic power. I never wish or will it to happen. It simply does and I don't have much control over it. I wouldn't consider that to be power."

Sheila laughed at the image I described, but continued to listen with great interest as I told her about the visions of Sheri Noland.

"The drawing that I gave you was a place I saw in one of these visions. I saw a young woman bound and gagged in the building and I drew the picture so I wouldn't forget the details. Since you've lived there a long time I thought you might recognize the place. I didn't know at the time I sketched the picture that the woman in the vision was Sheri Noland who was kidnapped last week."

Sheila's eyes widened in amazement.

"She's in danger and because of the vision somehow I have to help her."

Sheila let out a deep breath as though she had held it throughout my story. With compassion she said at last, "I can help you and I'm flattered that you would trust me with this. I have a very good friend who is a detective in Canton and he's very open-minded. His name is Cory Little and I trust him. I hope you will too. And I won't tell anyone what you've just said. They would think I was crazy."

She dialed the phone and told her friend the entire story leaving nothing out including the drawings' location her uncle had provided. When she hung up she smiled. "He wants us to drive up tomorrow morning and spend the day with him. He wants to take you to this area and have a look."

"How can I ever thank you Sheila for being an understanding friend and for not running out the door?" I said with a grin.

She laughed. "A thank you is not necessary. You would never have gone to all the trouble to tell me this story if it wasn't true. I could tell how difficult it was for you to share it. Besides, I'm looking forward to going tomorrow. I've never seen a psychic at work and it'll be nice to have a day off." She hugged me and laughed. Somewhat surprised by the hug, I left her office and almost fell running down the stairs.

I could hardly work the remainder of the day wanting to help find Sheri Noland as soon as possible, knowing from the visions the terror she felt. Search parties were being organized covering three counties, while the news media continued to broadcast reports of the abduction and details of the ongoing FBI and local police involvement, along with requesting any information from the public that might help them.

Early the next morning Sheila and I met at a gas station in Canton and we drove to the detective's office. His appearance took me by surprise. He was a gentle, young, good-looking man whose bright eyes were filled with wisdom rather than the hard, stern demeanor I expected and he expressed great concern as he spoke with Sheila. She made the introductions and with a firm handshake he made me feel at ease.

Detective Little was less formal than I expected dressed in well fitting jeans and a tee shirt that showed off his physique. He never took his eyes from mine as I recounted the story Sheila had told him.

"I want you to know that I've seen and worked with psychics before," he began. "I don't know whether I believe what I've seen but I'm not opposed to anything that might save a person's life.

I know that these kinds of experiences exist, like police officers and detectives have gut feelings or hunches, and they act on them. I've done it a million times myself. Let's get in my van and take a drive."

"Lynn, this is Detective Smith," he said motioning to a man who had appeared behind me. "He and I have a special interest in this case since it occurred in our county and he'll be going with us today. Sheila, you can ride in the back with Detective Smith and Lynn, you ride up front with me."

Detective Smith was a quiet, sulking man with cropped, blond hair and blue eyes. He nodded his head as Detective Little introduced us but said nothing. I couldn't quite determine if the look on his face displayed annoyance. I wondered what was bothering him. He watched me through squinting questioning eyes as though he did not seem to like the idea of working with a clairvoyant. Detective Little was quiet as we rode through the remote, wooded areas of the county. He glanced at me often but tried not to be obvious.

An intense energy filled the air; the kind that appears only in autumn and the sky was crisp and clear beneath the bright sun. Under other circumstances this would have been a remarkable day, but it was clouded by the vision of Sheri Noland, our reason for being here. The air inside the van felt heavy and oppressive. I knew it was not.

Apprehension filled me as we drove through the beautiful countryside and I concentrated on the array of color covering the rolling hills as a diversion. God's artistic beauty took away my breath when we passed a glistening lake reflecting the brilliance of the sun. A few miles further Detective Little stopped the van beside a trout stream. It's gentle, rippling water instilled peace as we sat in silence for a few moments before starting out again.

I've always loved autumn — the season of my birth. Autumn represents to me a life inspiring time. The earth is discarding the past, preparing for the peace and solitude of winter before bursting into new life with spring. This season held a very different meaning for Sheri Noland.

"Do you see anything or sense anything here?" Detective Little asked as we drove winding around country roads over hilly terrain.

I shook my head. "No, I'm sorry. Nothing yet."

The journey through the countryside began to seem endless when I saw it — the dirt clearing, a rusted, metal building, railroad tracks, woods, the valley. The vision had transformed into reality through my physical sight. Waves of nausea swept over me, and a cold sweat covered my entire body.

"Stop the van. Please stop the van. I have to get out. I can't breathe."

I opened the door before Detective Little could stop and ran from the van gasping for air. My knees buckled at the edge of the woods. I was going to throw up. With every ounce of willpower I possessed, I fought to gain control but could just point to the woods. The detectives began searching for anything that might tell them if Sheri Noland was there or had been there. After ten or fifteen minutes they returned to where I sat on the ground still trying to regain my composure. They found nothing.

"Let's take a walk, Lynn, if you're up to it," Detective Little said as he extended his hand to help me up. "Might make you feel better."

We walked down the graveled road and onto the pavement that curved around the woods and a few modest houses. The detective watched me.

"Not again. Not another one," I pleaded as the woods and the houses faded away. In their place was a parked car on the road beside the woods. Inside the trunk of the car was the same woman I had seen before in the visions, hands bound, mouth gagged. The expensive, white Town Car was out of place in this area. This type of car most often belonged to upper, middle class wealth but this one was indicative of money not refinement. The interior was gaudy as though every available option had been installed. It contained everything money could buy but with no thought of the sophistication that accompanies taste. The woman lay lifeless and pale. *Why can't I see the license plate?* The sunlight blackened as I fainted.

"Lynn, can you hear me? Are you all right?" Detective Little was drawling his concern as he shook me and wiped my face with his handkerchief.

"What happened? What did you see?"

He was very disturbed by my actions, and when I described the car his face turned ashen, but he made no comment. He studied my eyes with great apprehension then suggested that we continue our search. He continued to glance at me with a disturbed look on his face as if he knew something he was unwilling to share.

More woods, more unknown areas. I was tired but I knew this was necessary, and I continued to watch the terrain. An underlying feeling of evil in the midst of the beautiful scenery stroked my senses. I almost expected to hear dueling banjos echoing from a farmhouse porch at any time. We must have ridden several more hours without talking, everyone waiting and watching. The sun beginning to tire of the day shadowed its light in protest. We drove over a wooden, single-lane bridge and through a bend in the dirt road onto the maintenance path beside the railroad tracks.

"Hello, this is Detective Little. What time is the next train scheduled on track forty-three?" he asked the railroad station attendant on his mobile phone.

"None due for at least another hour, detective," said the attendant.

"What time do you have?" asked the detective.

After confirming the time Detective Little drove down the railroad maintenance path beside the tracks past a utility building. There it was — the valley on one side, the hill on the other. My eyes blurred and the nausea began rising in my throat again as a heavy band tightened around my chest, leaving me gasping for breath. I did not have to tell him this time. Detective Little stopped the van and rushed around to help me out and I began to feel some relief as the air started flowing into my lungs once again.

"My God, do you know where you are, Lynn?" Without giving me time to answer he continued. "This is the back side of the same woods where you sensed something earlier today. We've got something here."

He yelled to the other detective, "Let's go. Sheila, keep an eye on Lynn. She's pretty shaken."

They disappeared into the woods while Sheila and I waited, praying. *Please let them find her.* We could hear them shouting to each other in the distance, but we could not see them. After a long while they returned and Detective Little called the Sheriff's Department on his mobile phone to request that a search party be organized.

"I don't know what we've got here but there's something in this area. I've got a psychic here with me, and this is the second time today she's made a believer out of me."

"Now, Cory, how can you believe a psychic?" said a voice over the radio. "You know those people aren't for real. I wouldn't organize a search party on the word of one of those crazy people. Have you totally lost your mind?" the deputy dispatcher asked annoyed.

"I don't care what you would or wouldn't do. I know what I've seen today. I want that search party and I want them here when the sun comes up. It's getting too dark now for us to see anything, but tomorrow morning I want at least twenty people in these woods. Now get busy, deputy."

I looked at Detective Little and whispered, "Please don't call me a psychic. I'm not a psychic. I just see things that most people don't." I bowed my head. "It's not something I ever wanted to do."

CHAPTER EIGHT

Another day passed without word from the kidnapper, now five days since the abduction. The ransom had been paid, but Sheri Noland was not released, causing grave concern. Special Agent Arthur asked Larry to come to the FBI's office for further questioning.

"Don't take this the wrong way," the assistant agent said matter-of-factly. "Just normal procedure. We need for you to submit to a polygraph test Mr. Noland to clarify a few things."

"No problem," Larry said, his hands already beginning to sweat.

"Mr. Noland, if this investigation is to proceed with any amount of success, we must cover all the facts of your wife's kidnapping. You will be asked questions regarding everything you saw the night of the abduction. I want you to answer yes or no to each question." The assistant agent explained the procedure to Larry as required by law.

Larry knew it would look bad for him if he refused the polygraph test.

"I'm ready so let's get on with it," Larry said after signing the stipulation authorizing the FBI to perform the test, and to use the results in court should a trial ensue.

Larry was seated in a large, armed chair facing the wall in a closet size examination room. Two coiled black tubes were placed around his upper and lower chest to record respiratory responses. A blood pressure cuff was placed on his left upper arm that monitored heart rate, pulse and blood pressure. Last, but not least, two Velcro fingerplates were attached to the third and fifth fingers on his right hand that would record sweat produced from his sweat glands.

Changes in the body were monitored by these devices and

transmitted to the computer. The polygraph software recorded the changes as questions were answered. The monitor displayed four lines; the top two lines recorded upper and lower breathing patterns, the third line recorded sweat gland changes, and the bottom line recorded the heart rate and pulse. Each line was significant if it indicated deception. Any movement of the body displayed on the monitor, but was distinguishable as movement and marked accordingly by the examiner.

A polygraph test results in 90% - 94% accuracy, but two charts are necessary for accuracy readings. No proper names are allowed in the questioning for they invoke emotions that change the outcome of the results.

The assistant agent was a certified polygraph examiner with more than eight years experience. He had a knack for reading people, and most often knew within thirty minutes if the person was deceiving without even bothering to look at the graph recording. The examiner thought Larry's arrogance would undermine his credibility in any situation, but especially his answers to the questions.

Larry's heart rate was increasing as well as his blood pressure. Sweat began to bead on his forehead. The agent sat down behind him at a small desk that housed the computer causing Larry even more discomfort. He could feel the examiner's breath on his neck and he shivered uncontrollably. The agent reeked of Old Spice cologne and Larry's stomach churned.

"So, this is how a death row inmate would feel strapped in an electric chair," Larry said with a half-hearted chuckle. The agent frowned at his inept attempt at humor. Larry trembled and the graphs recorded his response.

"Don't move now. Let's test the accuracy of the responses with information that we already know about you. This part of the test is referred to as the acquaintance test. We use this to make adjustments if needed for interpretation. Answer yes or no to the questions. Don't elaborate on any answer. Ready? Is your name

Larry Noland?"

"Yes," Larry said keeping his eyes fixed on the blank wall before him.

"Do you live in Canton, Georgia?"

"Yes."

"Are you a lawyer by profession?"

"Yes."

The agent scrutinized Larry's responses as he fine-tuned the polygraph software, marking inconsistencies such as movement or pressure changes.

"Okay, looks good. Let's get started then. Did that man have a gun?"

"Yes."

"Was that man alone?"

"Yes."

"Was that man six feet tall?"

"Yes."

The testing continued for more than an hour while the examining agent kept watching the graphs in disbelief as they registered Larry's responses. According to the graphs, the only questions he had answered without deception were his name, address and occupation.

"We need to try a few more questions. There seems to be some sort of problem with the computer," stated the examining agent with a look of concern on his face.

"What's the problem? Can't you people get your shit together and quit wasting my time?" Larry shouted annoyed. Sweat was now dripping from his forehead. He was unable to see the computer monitor behind him and not knowing what it read was maddening.

"Just a minor adjustment is needed. Sorry for the inconvenience."

He adjusted the computer program and repeated the questions, but this time in random order. Again, the few questions answered without deception, according to the graphs, were his name, address and occupation.

Upon completion of the test, all the tubes, blood pressure cuff and fingerplates were removed from Larry's body while the examiner instructed him.

"Wait in here for a few minutes, Mr. Noland. I need to get some paperwork for Special Agent Arthur. Can I get you a cup of coffee or a soft drink?" The examiner escorted Larry to the waiting room adjacent to the examining room.

Larry grimaced and his eyes darted about the room. "No. How long is this going to take? I have clients who need my attention, and I need to get out of here. Damn it, I need to be out searching for my wife since the FBI can't seem to do anything right," Larry said as he glared at the agent.

"Shouldn't be but a few minutes. I'll be right back." He closed the door leaving Larry alone in the waiting room, and rushed down the hall to Special Agent Arthur's office, rapped on the door and bolted inside without waiting for an invitation.

"Sir, he's failed the polygraph test. I thought something was malfunctioning with the equipment, but that's not it. He isn't telling the truth."

"He may be telling the truth, but not everyone can pass a polygraph test. They get too nervous and the graphs can't register accurate responses. You know that."

"Sir, I don't want to disagree, but the graphs registered fine with irrelevant information. How could deception be indicated on the relevant and comparison questions if he is telling the truth? I've done hundreds of these tests and I know when someone is lying."

Special Agent Arthur scratched his head. "I'll decide later what to do about the test. We should have him show us how he got out of the duct tape before we let him go. Why don't you take care of that and call me when you've completed it?"

Not believing what he had just heard, the agent walked back

down the hall to find Larry pacing the room. The computer did not register half-truths.

"Mr. Noland, Special Agent Arthur wants you to show us exactly how your wife tied you with the duct tape," he said. "Can you do that?"

Larry's face turned scarlet, and the carotid arteries in his neck protruded. "You've wasted enough of my time with this bullshit. I'm leaving. Don't you think I've been through enough? Am I a suspect in this case? If I am, you better read my Miranda rights and arrest me or let me leave now."

The agent shook his head. "No, sir, you're not a suspect at this time, but we have to check out everything. We wouldn't be doing our job otherwise, and you wouldn't like that either. Here's a roll of duct tape. Tell me how she tied you and I'll place the tape on you. As soon as we complete this you're free to go."

Seeing that he had no choice without appearing uncooperative and suspicious, Larry began to tell the agent how to tie him. Once he had finished binding Larry's arms and legs, he taped his eyes and mouth, and then called Special Agent Arthur on the intercom to join them.

"Okay, now show us how you got out of the tape, Mr. Noland," commanded Special Agent Arthur.

Larry maneuvered his body trying to free himself of the duct tape, twisting and contorting like a figure from the Gumby cartoon. A grin worked its way across the agent's face in spite of the seriousness of this test. He turned his head away so that his boss would not see his face.

Larry worked his arms free first taking a long time. He tore the tape off his face and at last off his legs. His face and arms were red and irritated when he completed his task. Hair from his head and arms was stuck to the duct tape.

Satisfied, Special Agent Arthur told Larry that he was free to leave the building once he had signed the computer printout indicating that he knew the results of the polygraph test. He walked down the hall back to his office, closed the door, and rubbed his forehead. His head was pounding. *Damn, now we have no choice but to ignore the results of the failed polygraph tests. How could he free himself from the duct tape like that?*

After Noland left the building, the agent burst into Special Agent Arthur's office.

"Sir, shouldn't we compare the test duct tape with the actual crime scene duct tape?"

"Yes but we can't do that," said Arthur annoyed at the agent's question.

"But sir, why not?"

"The crime scene tape was thrown away by mistake." Special Agent Arthur shook his head and narrowed his eyes. "Some damn idiot didn't put it in the evidence room as instructed and it got tossed. Now go do your job and quit telling me how to do mine," he shouted pointing a thick finger at the agent. "And, don't say a word about this to anyone else. Understand?"

"Sir, I'm sorry, but I have one more question."

Arthur looked up at his assistant. *Why can't this man just leave things alone? He never knows when to stop asking questions.*

"What about the eyewitness who saw a woman sitting in a Jeep the night Sheri Noland was kidnapped? The witness thought it was around ten o'clock and that her eyes were covered. Even if he did not remember what street he was on, how many Jeeps are there in that neighborhood? It's not that big. Shouldn't we consider his testimony as significant evidence that Larry Noland might have had something to do with the abduction?" He looked at Special Agent Arthur with a steady, determined glare as though challenging his superior. "I think that testimony is too important to ignore. Don't you?"

Arthur inhaled and stared at his probing agent. He thought carefully before giving his answer. "We have covered everything we need to cover with respect to Larry Noland at this time." His voice slow and calm, he continued, "Once again, I will remind you that I am the agent in charge of this investigation. I will decide who gets questioned, when they are questioned, and what questions are asked. You've brought up some important facts and I'll take them under consideration. We're finished here for now. You're excused."

* * * *

Larry left the FBI's office shaking with rage. Failing the polygraph test was not acceptable and he was furious with himself. He had just placed himself on the FBI's probable suspect list, and the partners would not be happy about that. But, he rationalized, he had gotten himself out of the duct tape and that must have confused the hell out of the FBI. They never expected him to pull that off. He still was not sure how he accomplished it, but it proved a point and the FBI would have to take that into consideration.

Larry felt better about his situation as he drove back to his office, and dismissed the entire ordeal by the time he pulled into the parking lot. One test cancelled out the other, so the FBI was back to square one. They could not prove anything, and in Larry's opinion, none of them were smart enough to trap him.

He got out of his car humming a tune as though he did not have a care in the world, and walked with brazen confidence into the firm's building.

CHAPTER NINE

Family, friends, even strangers awaited news of Sheri Noland's whereabouts after the ransom was paid, but none came. Day after agonizing day passed and there was no call from the kidnapper, only the heaviness of silence remained.

Sarah and Wayne Hilliard with their younger daughter, Beth, moved into a local hotel unable to bear the chaos in Sheri's home. News reporters, Larry's friends and family were in and out of the Noland house in a steady stream. Katherine Noland moved into her son's house not wanting to be left out of anything. She thrived on the attention given to her by the media, never missing an opportunity to loudly express herself to whoever would listen.

Her husband was not often seen at his son's house, nor was he concerned about the FBI's and local police officer's handling of this kidnapping. They knew what to do. He wanted solitude in his own house away from all these people, and he especially wanted to not hear his wife's constant chatter. He was tired of pretending and he didn't care what was happening to his daughter-in-law.

Sarah sat by the window in the sterile hotel room, staring out onto the busy street below. The first rain in weeks began to trickle down the windowpane, mimicking her tears. She despised this town. It had taken her daughter from her and she would never forgive it. Words of sympathy from the town's residents only seemed to mask the evil that controlled it. Sarah shivered with a coldness that bore its way through her bones, climbed up her limbs and spread over her torso. Thoughts of Sheri being tortured or killed crept into her mind in spite of her efforts to keep them away. She turned away from the rain-splattered window, and with hollowed eyes looked at her husband's face. She thought he looked old. Sensing her need, Wayne walked across the room and sat down beside her on the hard bed.

"Our baby. Oh Wayne, why would anyone want to take her?" she asked knowing that he had no answer. "I don't understand. Why didn't Larry do something to stop that man?" She angrily sobbed as she laid her head on her husband's chest and clung to him.

"Damn him," she shouted. "How could he let someone take her? I've never trusted him. I've always felt that he did not love Sheri. He's always thought only of himself."

Wayne tried to console his wife. He stroked her hair and held her in his arms. They searched each other's eyes for strength as they tried to understand why someone would want to hurt their beautiful daughter. The sky continued to shed tears as though it felt their sorrow.

"Wayne, do you remember when Sheri was a teenager?" she asked, as though remembering would ease the pain. "Sheri had seen an article in the newspaper describing a child's terminal illness, and she wrote a condolence letter to the family."

Wayne nodded his head without speaking. Sarah continued, "Things like that touched Sheri in a way we couldn't possibly understand, and she didn't even know those people. She was a joy in everyone's life. Why would anyone take such a special person from us?"

"I don't know, Sarah," he whispered, shaking his head. He had no answers for her. Lost in his own tormented thoughts, he stood again and stared out the window.

Autumn had not brought cold weather, but Sarah felt a strange chill, one mixed with hot rage. Until now she had never known hate, but she felt an uncontrollable hatred for the people who imprisoned her precious daughter, and she wanted to strike out. She turned back to the window and continued to stare into the rain, her eyes dull and glazed.

Wayne paced the floor cursing the people responsible for taking his daughter, while at the same time, pleading with God to return Sheri safely. His mind was crazed with the anger he felt and the helplessness to which he refused to surrender, even as his frustration mounted. He had to find her.

* * * *

Yards of wires, recording devices, and agents had been removed from the Noland house. A temporary office was set up in town because there was no need for further activity at the house. The kidnapper had not called. The investigation continued as agents checked out leads and evidence with the help of the local police and sheriff's departments.

Sheri's family offered a one hundred-thousand dollar reward to any person or persons who would give them information leading to Sheri's safe return, but their plea seemed to fall on deaf ears. Hundreds of concerned friends, morbid curiosity seekers, and compassionate strangers searched the woods that encompassed a three-county area, praying with each step that they would find her.

The FBI offered a ten thousand dollar reward for information leading to the recovery of the Nolands' Jeep taken in the kidnapping. It had not been located and authorities thought it might contain valuable clues as to Sheri's whereabouts.

Out of desperation, the FBI began broadcasting portions of the taped ransom demand through the media, hoping someone would recognize the kidnapper's voice. The calls poured in.

"I've heard the tape and I know who that man is," one caller claimed without identifying himself.

"I know who he is and I know where he lives," claimed another anonymous caller. "There's no doubt that it's him."

FBI and local authorities immediately began checking out the leads. The alleged kidnapper was Daniel Spicer, identified by dozens of callers, all anonymous. He lived in Canton not far from the Noland residence. The man had no criminal record, but was known to be rather unscrupulous. Everyone in the area knew he had money problems.

Agents drove to the Spicer home to question him and his wife, Donna. Hours of questioning led them to believe that he was hiding something. They had no viable evidence, but dozens of callers who refused to identify themselves knew something, and it was the FBI's responsibility to find out what.

Believing there might be a potential break in the case, the Hilliards and Larry Noland were called to the FBI's temporary headquarters. Special Agent Arthur, accompanied by his assistants, discussed Spicer and his probable involvement in the kidnapping.

"We need to get a search warrant," said Special Agent Arthur, as if thinking out loud. "We'll need the local judge to issue it because we know Spicer hasn't taken Sheri across a state line."

"Sir, how do we know that he hasn't taken her across a state line?" asked the assistant agent.

"We just know that he hasn't," snapped Arthur.

"We have reason to believe the suspect might be suicidal, so we'll keep constant surveillance on him. I've already made arrangements for local officers to watch his house around the clock. We'll assist if necessary. We can't arrest him until we have evidence, and we must have the search warrant in order to get it," he told them.

"If Spicer is suicidal take him into custody immediately," Wayne Hilliard demanded. "We have to find out where he took Sheri. She's been missing for six days. What more do you want for God's sake?"

"We can't do that at this time," Arthur said. "We must obtain the search warrant first, and then find some kind of incriminating evidence before we can even take him in for further questioning."

"We can't take the chance of him dying of suicide before we find Sheri," Sarah Hilliard said. "Damn it, you can at least take the man into protective custody. You don't need a search warrant to do that.

Can't you hold him for seventy-two hours and keep an eye on him?"

"I'm sorry, ma'am. We can't do that right now," said Special Agent Arthur. "We'll get the warrant and then we can do this the right way. We have to follow proper procedure. You wouldn't want his case to be thrown out of court on a technicality because we didn't arrest him properly, would you?"

"He'll never make it to court for you to worry about a technicality if he kills himself first," Sarah yelled.

That afternoon a local judge issued the search warrant based on probable cause, and a team of FBI agents and local law enforcement officers swarmed Daniel Spicer's house. They were ruthless as they tore through each room, searching for anything and everything that could be used against him.

Spicer's family stood in the living room watching in fear and shock as the intruders destroyed their home, while they in turn were being watched. In one room books were tossed onto the floor with their pages torn and curled. Clothes were thrown in disarray as closets were torn apart in another. Beds were stripped; mattresses and pillows ripped open, stuffing filling the air. Dishes were broken, and pots and pans clanked as they were tossed about in the kitchen. Groceries in the pantry were emptied onto the floor, cans were bent, jars broken. Pictures were torn off the walls, their linings ripped open and discarded with no concern for damage. Sofa cushions were sliced apart and thrown wherever they landed. Contents of drawers were dumped onto the floors. Some items were discarded as useless while others were bagged and labeled as evidence, and taken into custody. When the search was over, the house was in shambles much like the life of the Spicer family. But Spicer was not arrested.

* * * *

The day following the search, Daniel Spicer, still in his home but visibly shaken, gathered his family together in their living room.

"I can't say what's going on. They'll kill me if I do, and maybe all of you. If you find a suicide note and I'm dead, look for the son-of-a-bitch who killed me. I wouldn't do it to myself. There's cocaine involved and these are powerful people. That's all I can say for now." Spicer then called his lawyer because he knew what would come next, and he feared the police and the FBI. Knowing what these people were capable of doing to him, he needed protection, someone who could help him. A lawyer could hear the entire story, but not repeat it to anyone. Daniel knew about lawyer-client privileged information, and the lawyer would tell him what he should do. They set up an appointment for the following day.

Spicer's wife, Donna, had stayed with him through all his ups and downs. His heart surgery coming at their lowest financial point had almost broken her spirit. Now this.

"How could you get involved with drug dealing? You know how dangerous that is, Daniel. It's only been a few weeks since your surgery, and getting upset is going to cause you to have a relapse. You know the doctor said you had to take it easy and not get stressed. You're still very weak. What are you trying to do to yourself and to us?"

He knew she was right, but he did not want to hear about it right now. He had enough problems — things she could not begin to know, things he could never tell her.

While Spicer remained in his home, local law enforcement officers kept the house under surveillance, and the FBI continued to debate the charges on which they would arrest him. There were several options based on the evidence they had obtained, but they could not decide which one to use. Agents had found a pair of Spicer's work boots hidden in the closet under a blanket. The sole matched a print found in the soft earth beside the Noland's house, but they needed to find the money. Special Agent Arthur tried to convince the Hilliards that they had no choice. Real evidence was needed to get a full conviction for Spicer.

Two days passed while the FBI debated the issues, and Sheri's family became more distressed at the thought of Daniel ending his life. He was their only link to the whereabouts of their daughter. They might never find her if he killed himself.

Spicer's family helped him move the mattress from his bed into the living room. He insisted that his family all sleep together on the floor. It was safer in the center of the house because he could see the doorways and windows around him. He knew the house was being watched by local law enforcement, but few could be trusted. Many of the department's officers were involved in the syndicate's illegal drug trafficking, a way of subsidizing their income. He was sure they worked for the same people who had hired him for the kidnapping, and they weren't about to let him talk. His one hope was that a few of the police watching his house would protect him. He did not know about the FBI, their reputation was always bad, and he had heard rumors that many of their agents were on the syndicates' payroll.

"No one could get through all the cops out there so we're safe for now," Spicer quietly told his family as he turned out the lights, trying to console not only them but himself as well.

Sleep eluded him. His mind would not turn itself off. As he lay in the darkness he wondered what had happened to Sheri Noland after he left her at the mine. He had no further contact with the others after that. He could not risk it with the FBI hanging around his house. The only person who had been paid for their part in the kidnapping was Ann Weisman. He had handed over her share of the money a couple of days after he received the ransom so she would leave him alone. The remainder was well hidden, and only one of the others knew where. He could not touch his share until this was over.

* * * *

Detective Little continued to search the wooded area that Lynn had shown him a few days earlier. He knew she had seen or felt something in that area and he had to find out what she knew. Even though he had not really believed in psychic experiences before then, she had convinced him. He searched the woods again because his gut feeling kept telling him something was there. The search party had scrutinized the woods and found nothing, yet he knew something was there.

He recalled Lynn's reactions and thought about where they were each time she had exhibited the strange behavior. He remembered the graveled road and began walking toward it hoping his instincts would reveal something.

* * * *

A young girl, who lived in the same area of town as Daniel Spicer, wandered away from her apartment while playing. She saw a plastic box on the ground beside the garbage dumpster and curiously picked it up and examined it. She ran back to her apartment to show it to her dad. He placed the cassette tape into the player thinking his daughter had found a music cassette. Instead, he heard voices talking, plotting a kidnapping. The voices on the tape referred to prominent people in the area, and it reminded him of actors rehearsing their lines. The male voice was the same voice that had been broadcast on radio and television in connection with the Sheri Noland kidnapping. But there was a female voice as well. The little girl's father immediately called the FBI to report his find, and when they arrived at his apartment, he turned it over to them.

The FBI confirmed that the voice was indeed Daniel Spicer's. References to places, family and other information on the tape, led the FBI to believe that they also knew the identity of the female voice. This was the break they had been hoping for. They drove to her house, which was across the street from the wooded area Detective Little had been searching. When she saw the FBI at her door, Ann Weisman broke down and told them everything.

"I only did what I was told to do," Ann said after she heard the tape. "He made me do it. Where did you get that tape anyway?"

"Who made you do what?" an agent asked.

"Daniel Spicer. He said he would pay me ten thousand dollars to hold that Noland girl in the woods while he collected the ransom money. He was really pissed when her husband didn't get the ransom money to him the first night. He came after her the next day and tore out of the woods. I didn't know what he would do. I've never seen him so pissed off before."

"Where did he take her Ms. Weisman?" Special Agent Arthur asked.

"I got no idea," she said, shaking her head. "He didn't tell me nothing. He just left with her and said they were going to get her husband for being so stupid. He was really mad. He didn't tell me nothing else. My job was to keep her until he got the money and came after her, that's all. Kinda like babysitting, you know?""You said 'they were going to get her husband,' Ms. Weisman. Who are they? Are there other people involved besides you and Daniel Spicer?"

"No. I just meant Daniel and me," she said, irritated for letting that slip.

"You don't know where Daniel took Sheri Noland?" Special Agent Arthur asked once more.

"No. He told me a few days later that he took her to the woods and let her go. I'll sign a confession if that's what you want. I didn't hurt that Noland girl. I never saw her again after Spicer took her, I swear."

"Ms. Weisman," she was informed, " you are under arrest for the kidnapping of Sheri Noland."

As they handcuffed her and seated her in the car, Special Agent Arthur gruffly read her Miranda rights.

Ann Weisman was driven to the local jail and placed in protective, maximum custody. No one, especially Sheri Noland's family, was allowed to speak with her.

* * * *

Two men, one with dark, stringy hair and a beard, the other one large with sandy hair, recovered the Nolands' Jeep a few days later. They claimed they were hunting in the woods one county from the Nolands' residence, and stumbled across the Jeep. Both men lived in a town fifteen miles away and both had dubious reputations. The bearded man had known Spicer in the past, possibly work related in mine exploration. Local deputies questioned the two men, but let them go. According to the deputies, there was no evidence that either man was involved in the kidnapping of Sheri Noland or the theft of the Jeep.

The Jeep had been wiped clean, no fingerprints or clues were present. Even though there had been little rain in the past two weeks, the Jeep had no dust on it and appeared to have been sheltered. A local truck driver who drove a route daily through the area, told deputies that he knew it had not been there all the time because he stopped there every day to rest. Whoever had possession of the Jeep had placed it there after the reward was offered. The authorities completely discounted the driver's testimony.

* * * *

Daniel Spicer watched over his family as they slept. Feeling the devastation he had caused, he prophetically knew at that moment his life would soon be over. This knowing was clearer than anything he had ever experienced in his life. They would kill him. He finally understood — he was their scapegoat. How could he ever have been so stupid? The law would not protect him. Why should they? Too many of them were involved in the cocaine operation. There was no one he could trust, not even the lawyer he had hired to help him.

He needed to get his family out of this house, out of this town where they would be safe, especially his daughters. His wife and daughters were important to him, and he knew he had miserably failed them. He had not been able to provide for them as he wanted, no matter what he tried to do. They all deserved better than this, but especially his daughters who were young, impression-able, and he did not want them to ever become involved in drug trafficking or something worse. What a horrible father he had been exposing them to this. He knew they would have a difficult time if he did not make it through. If? Who was he kidding? There was no if. He should have known better than to trust these people. He should have thought about his family before he had agreed to become involved. He knew in his gut that something would go wrong, but he was desperate for money. When the others had talked about the kidnapping, they had made it sound so simple.

He slipped another nitroglycerin tablet under his tongue and closed his eyes to wait.

When Spicer's family awoke, he insisted that they leave the house immediately assuring them that it was for their safety, and that he would be all right. The weight of guilt on his shoulders bore heavily as he watched them pack their bags and prepare to leave. Spicer stood at the front door and held them as long as he dared before making them leave. He knew this was the last time he would ever see them. He patted his wife's cheek as a gesture of his love. Unable to speak for fear that the tears would come Spicer watched his fam-ily leave through the maze of police officers watching his house. He wondered if this was how the Hilliards felt. This hopelessness. They would never see their daughter again, he was sure of it, and he was the instrument of destruction, at least in part.

He choked back the tears and reached into his pocket for a nitro-glycerin tablet as he felt the pressure mounting in his chest. He knew his family would be questioned again, but they did not know enough to cause any real damage to themselves. It was better this way for all of them. He walked back into his house, closed the door behind him, and began walking through each room as though he was seeing it for the last time. He felt empty inside — just like his house. In all the years he had lived there he had never seen or heard crows in his backyard, and yet today, the ground was covered in black. Spicer shivered and felt the day of reckoning fast approaching.

CHAPTER TEN

Without a sound he opened the back door of the house, sneaked in and began to make his way toward the living room where Daniel Spicer slept alone on the floor. The faint glow of a nightlight cast dark, disproportionate shadows across the floor. He passed by the mahogany staircase, paused for a moment at the bottom step, and imagined Spicer's two young, beautiful daughters upstairs asleep, but he knew Spicer was alone in the house. The floor planks moaned with each step as if they knew why he was there. The noise woke Spicer. Trembling, he squinted into the gloom unable to see the source of the sound. Time ceased to exist. Breath stopped. He knew they would come for him so he had waited not knowing what else to do. He now thought about running, but he did not have the strength to get up off the floor, and without his glasses his world was a blur. He could not reach them on the table without getting up and he dared not move. Helpless and weary, he waited.

I'm going to die now. The thought came as a simple matter of fact and seemed to ricochet inside his head. He knew it. The air held death. His body felt it.

The moaning stopped. The dark figure let out a long sigh and leaned over Spicer without speaking. The room transformed into a silent tomb with his thudding pulse the only sound.

"You shouldn't a screwed up you stupid son-of-a-bitch. We was countin' on you. All you had to do was git the money the first day. We woulda taken care of the rest. You made a lot of people what I'd call it, nervous, by runnin' around all over town makin' phone calls."

Daniel's heart pounded with a paralyzing fear that gripped his body. He grasped the corner of the sheet with white knuckles, his body taut. He could not move. The raspy, thick voice sounded strangely familiar and Daniel tried to force himself to picture the face.

"I did what they told me to do. I didn't screw up," he choked on his whispered words.

He thought about running again, but he could not get away. Daniel knew his own failing heart would attack him before this demon could kill. *What irony.*

"Here's a pen and some paper. You write a suicide note. Write it to anybody. I don't give a damn who. Write it jest like I'm a tellin' you or we'll git your family too, 'specially those perty, young daughters."

Spicer was not a religious man, but at the mention of harm to his family, he bowed his head and silently prayed for God to protect them. He did not ask for himself; he knew God would only laugh at him.

"My glasses." Spicer motioned with his head to the table where they lay. The dark figure handed them to him and pulled him upright on the floor.

In the eerie silence of the darkened room, the intruder's raspy voice began to recite Spicer's final words. He turned on a flashlight so he could see and Spicer watched his own shaking hand write the words in the circle of light as it glared on his trifocals. He confessed to all things, some real, some not; his involvement in a drug deal, his three accomplices including a man with long, blond, stringy hair. The garbled scenario explained the presence of money in his house as a payoff in drug trafficking. He apologized to his family, but never once did he mention the kidnapping or the whereabouts of Sheri Noland just as he was instructed. He signed his name illegibly.

"Let's git the money now and this'll all be over," said the raspy voice.

Daniel's fear took on a life of its own. He detached his mind from his body as though he was another person observing his actions. He watched himself walk across the room to the cabinet. He watched his hand open the hidden drawer. He saw himself take out the banded stacks of bills and hand them to the dark figure. His executioner placed hundreds of dollars around the living room. Spicer strained his eyes attempting to see the man's face in the darkened room, but to no avail. The stench of stale beer and chewing tobacco permeated the air and he gagged. When the dark figure shoved him onto a chair, a flicker of light bounced off the floor and over the gold tips of the man's boots. Spicer recognized the boots — the hired killer — the kidnapping.

He watched the events taking place in his living room as though he was no part of it. In disbelief he watched the killer place the rifle on the floor at his feet, the barrel pointing up toward his body. Spicer's mouth opened as if to say something in protest and then closed without uttering a sound.

"It's been nice doin' business with you." He squeezed the trigger. Spicer saw his killer's face melt in the brilliant light then fade into nothingness.

The dark figure leisurely strolled out the back door. He placed some of the money in Spicer's truck parked behind the house then walked away through the woods completely unnoticed.

An FBI agent and a local police officer sat in an unmarked car parked at the end of the short street adjacent to the front of Spicer's modest house. Perched on a hill with large trees behind it, the house was partially hidden from the street. It was impossible for the officer and agent to see all angles of the house from their location. They heard the gunshot around four thirty in the morning, but remained inside the car. "What the hell was that?" the agent asked the officer. "Did you hear that?"

"Sounded like a gunshot to me. Maybe the bastard killed himself. Let's just wait awhile. Might not have even been a gunshot. I'm not going in there to see."

"How long does it take a body to bleed to death after a gunshot?"

"A few hours, I think. Let's just wait. Maybe the neighbors will call it in and if dispatch sends a patrol car we won't have to bother."

Two and one-half hours after they heard the gunshot they radioed for backup.

"Dispatch this is 221. We just heard a gunshot coming from the stakeout location. Request for backup immediately. 10-4."

"221, I copy. Backup's on the way. Do not proceed until backup arrives. I repeat do not proceed. You copy?"

"We copy. We're staying put."

They waited for backup and after three police cars arrived, the officers broke through Daniel Spicer's front door. They found him dead of a single gunshot wound to the chest. Lying on the floor beside him was a blood-splattered suicide note along with a rifle.

CHAPTER ELEVEN

CANTON, GA. (A.P.) — A suspect in the kidnapping-for-ransom of a 25 year-old Canton woman killed himself today as FBI agents staked out his home.

A Canton woman, Ann Weisman, who agreed to cooperate with authorities and testify against the suspect, Daniel Spicer, was charged with first-degree kidnapping, said District Attorney Donald Butcher.

Butcher said authorities found about $200,000 that was believed to have been part of the ransom paid by relatives of Sheri Noland. The money was discovered in Spicer's house by FBI and local authorities after his body was found.

A search for Mrs. Noland continues today, Butcher said.

After talking with Mrs. Weisman, Butcher said, "We knew beyond all doubt that Daniel Spicer was the man responsible for the kidnapping of Mrs. Noland."

Sitting on the sofa in my den absorbed in the news broadcasts of the continuing search for Sheri Noland, I thought I heard the whisper of a woman's voice.

"Go north, Lynn. You must go north."

"North of what?" I said out loud and looked around to see who was speaking. There was no one in the room. *I'm working too hard and it's getting the best of me. Now I'm hearing voices.* I shrugged it off and went back to watching the news broadcasts.

The faces on the television screen began to dissolve and I could see a paved, two-lane road. On either side of the road I saw large, concrete water drainage tiles, and a road sign with the number 2, then a rusted non-legible number followed by the number 9. Beyond the sign was an old, decomposed farmhouse, its roof now fallen to the floor.

The vision continued — an abandoned timber site off to one side of the paved road. The area was muddy. Behind the cleared timber site was nothing but woods. My hands began to tremble and my breath was coming in short gasps. I saw a bearded man with dark, stringy, long hair wearing heavy gold necklaces around his neck holding a snubbed-nose gun. His face wore a sneer as though he was taunting someone. At his side stood a heavyset person with extremely broad shoulders and sandy hair. This person appeared to be turned sideways as though looking behind the man holding the gun. I could not see the face nor could I determine if the person was male or female. My eyes followed the gun and I could see that it was pointed down toward the ground, pointed at a young, brunette woman lying in the mud with a look of both astonishment and terror on her face.

I felt rather strange, light-headed, faint, and the room seemed to be spinning. What was happening to me? Paralyzed, I realized that it was now me looking up at the gun and that I was lying on the ground. But it could not be me. It was as though I had taken her place, was seeing through her eyes and feeling her terror, but why? How? I did not understand this at all.

I wanted to scream out. It's not me! It's her! The reasoning portion of my mind began to take over perhaps as a protective mechanism. I attempted to rationalize this strange experience because this was not possible even in clairvoyant visions. I was supposed to be an observer of the vision, not personally experiencing it. This had to be a delusion. As I looked at the muzzle of the gun I knew that life would soon be over, but over for me or for Sheri?

The vision faded away and I sat on the sofa trembling, soaked in sweat, screaming, "I don't want to do this. Please God, stop these visions."

* * * *

The search continued for Sheri Noland. A month had passed since the kidnapping yet every television station within a hundred miles of Canton was continuing to broadcast news of the search parties. Larry Noland was shown only a few times participating in the searches, his mother always by his side. She never missed an opportunity to smile at the camera or voice her opinion. Larry never responded to questions asked by the reporters, but the look on his face answered. Hostility. Annoyance. Void of grief. Sarah, Wayne and Beth Hilliard accompanied by students from Emory University, friends and family members were always present.

I worked diligently attempting to block the visions I had begun to detest. I forced my mind to concentrate on anything that was not connected to Sheri Noland, and if she tried to sneak into my thoughts, I quickly dispelled her. I wanted no part of this. It was taking its toll on my health both physically and mentally. I could not sleep or eat or concentrate on my job. Something had to stop this madness and stop it soon, but was I the only one who could stop it or was it already too late?

Most of the time I was in awe of this ability, but these days I was terribly afraid of it. I remembered struggling with the intense emotions connected to this ability when I was younger, until finally, I reached a point in my life where I knew I had to accept this gift for whatever purpose it served. It would not go away. My greatest challenge was a spiritual one. I had grown up in a strict Southern Baptist family, but I was fortunate to have a mother and an older sister who also had a clairvoyant gift even though they suppressed it most of the time. In our minister's opinion, clairvoyance was a contradiction to all the Church believed. He viewed this ability as a threat to God's teachings, but I did not agree with him. He quoted Bible scripture from the Old Testament about the sin of calling up spirits and conversing with them. I assured him that I was not calling anyone and if I did, it would be by telephone. The gift of seeing was an instrument to help others. It certainly was not meant to harm them. I reminded him that God worked in mysterious ways and perhaps this was just one example.

I believed that everyone had a purpose in life, and even though I questioned this so-called gift, I knew it was an honorable part of my life based on my experiences thus far. I was not a fortune teller; I could not tell people what would happen in their future, nor did I read palms or cards, but visions were as much a part of my senses as physical hearing and sight. My inner turmoil continued each time I had a vision, but I would always ask God for guidance, and I would try to use this sight for a higher purpose, never personal gain. But now weary and worn, I wanted these visions to stop plaguing me.

* * * *

The soft, commanding voice I heard weeks before again whispered, "Lynn, go north. Won't you help me?"

Why? Why? Why couldn't she leave me alone? I could not run from the visions and I could not ignore her no matter how much I tried. I was trapped.

I located a state of Georgia road map and began searching for roads near Canton that had the numbers 2 and 9 in them. Just south of Canton — 249, the only road that had those numbers in any sequence on the entire map. That did not confirm the information in the vision though. All states utilize the same numbering system for their county or state roads I thought, but I had to know.

I got into my car and followed the map until I located the county road even though the sky was churning into gray, curdled milk and threatening rain. Turning onto the road I began to drive *north* when approximately ten miles further I could see large, concrete, drain tiles on either side of the road. Construction was about to begin on the road and the tiles were placed one after the other. My heart rate accelerated as I realized the tiles were the same size and in the same location as I had seen in the vision.

Captivated by the surroundings I drove further searching the area. I felt the weight of the air outside my car bearing down as if trying to paralyze my efforts. I shivered for no apparent reason. A short distance ahead I saw a road sign, the first one visible since I had turned onto County Road 249. It was battered and rusted and difficult to read. I could drive no further. I stopped the car on the road's shoulder, turned off the engine and took a deep breath slowly letting out the air. The sign mirrored the one in my vision including the rusted middle number. Just past the sign stood an old, dilapidated farmhouse. Cold chills spiraled up my spine spreading icy fingers over my entire body. With trembling hands I placed a cassette into the tape player, turned up the volume as loud as I dared, and surrounded myself with "The Alleluia Chorus."

I sat for a very long time staring at the rusted sign, completely in awe that another part of the vision had transformed into reality. I think it was in these moments that I began to fully understand that Sheri was indeed guiding me. But I could not understand what this county road had to do with her. I did not have enough information to fit the pieces together in any order so that they made sense to me. There had to be more. The sky suddenly parted like the Red Sea and huge dollops of rain began to fall. I turned up the music, louder, louder.

* * * *

The first of many telephone calls came three days after I drove up

County Road 249, a female voice, quiet and subdued. I was standing in my kitchen clearing away the dinner remains.

"Lynn, I'm calling on behalf of the judge. He asked me to call and warn you that you're in danger if you continue to search for Sheri Noland. You need to stay away from that area."

"Who are you?"

"It doesn't matter who I am. The judge is quite concerned that you have stumbled onto something you don't want to be a part of. He suggests that you stop now and get on with your life. Leave the search for the experts."

I sat down at the kitchen table puzzled by the phone call and gazed out the bay window. The sun was setting behind the trees and I watched the colors fade, wondering about this warning from a judge. How did he know who I was and how did he have access to my unpublished phone number? How did he know about the county road? I had told no one about the visions except my family, Sheila and Detective Little, and I felt confident that none of those people would betray me.Unnerved by the telephone call, but even more so by the extraordinary experience in the last vision, I needed answers. The following morning I called Dr. Arnold, a professor at the University of West Florida who was an expert in the field of parapsychology. I had read many of his articles on paranormal experiences and knew he was a source of explanation. I told him about my strange experience.

"Lynn, when psychic sight such as yours places you in the victim's standing, it means you are discovering the truth about what happened." His voice was soothing.

"I don't understand."

"You are being guided by the victim and she is showing you through these visions what happened. You must trust your ability and not get emotionally involved. Remember you are just an observer. You are not a part of these events."

"But why did I see the gun from her eyes? Why was I lying on the ground?"

"She's trying to tell you what she has experienced and where she is. You've become so attuned to her anguish you're becoming one person. You must separate yourself right now or you could be in real trouble from a mental perspective. The next time you have a vision remember you are only observing the events as they took place. If you become emotionally involved again you might stop the flow of visions. You don't want that to happen if you're to help find her. Trust yourself."

I thanked Dr. Arnold for his advice, but I didn't feel any better although now I was beginning to understand. I did not want to take Sheri's place in order to know how she felt or what she saw. But if I stayed emotionally involved the visions would stop and this madness would go away forever, or would it? I did not want to be personally involved. It was one thing to watch a vision, but quite another to be actually experiencing it. My brief episode of being in Sheri's place was horrifying. Dr. Arnold said she was guiding me, but I had already determined that when I saw the rusted road sign.

* * * *

Days passed without incident. I tried to concentrate on a normal life centered around work, family and making new friends, but I simply could not get the county road out of my mind. I kept seeing the road sign and the concrete tiles, Sheri Noland lying on the ground staring up at the gun, but most of all, the sneer on the bearded man's face as he taunted her. I felt someone or something was urging me to continue searching. I fought to stop it but it was stronger than I. I returned to County Road 249 against my better judgment.

In a rather disconcerting way Sheri was becoming my friend. I could feel what she had felt. I could see what she had seen. I knew what it was like to be on the ground facing a gun that was waiting to take away life. She continued to reach out to me, and each time she did we became more united. This need to help her, to find her, was becoming obsessive and I felt her presence growing stronger each time I tried to block the visions. Where was she taking me? What were these visions doing to my mind?

The second call came late in the night.

"Lynn, the judge says you must stop. You cannot continue with this search. You're going to be hurt and he doesn't want anyone else to be hurt," said the quiet, subdued woman's voice.

"What possible danger could there be in my driving along a public road?" I asked. "How does the judge know me and why won't he call me himself if he's so concerned?"

"He's filled with remorse over what happened to that little Noland girl, and he doesn't want anyone else to get hurt. How he knows about you is not important. Please take his warning seriously."

I had had enough of these calls. The next time, if there were a next time, I would trace it. I was growing weary of this invasion into my life and my privacy. I walked through my house peering out the windows and into the night, searching, and wondering who was watching me.

"Who was on the phone?" Jon asked as I finally settled down on the sofa beside him.

"It was the woman calling on behalf of the judge again. I do not understand why she's calling. If the judge is so concerned why doesn't he call me?" I said as I snuggled up to a blanket.

"Why would she call him 'judge' if he doesn't want you to know who he is?" Jon asked.

"Sounds to me like he does want me to know," I said.

"Lynn, you have to stop this," Jon said with great concern. "You have tapped into something very dangerous, and I don't want you or anyone in our family to get hurt. Your visions have always worried me, but this one is the worst. Please for your safety and ours, stay out of it. You cannot bring her back and you know she's dead by now. Getting yourself killed isn't going to help anyone."

I raised my eyebrows and gave him a questioning look.

"I'm gone so much of the time and I worry about you. Don't you know that?" he said lovingly as he took my hand in his.

Jon was right, but the phone calls, the visions, and Sheri's voice haunted me and would not let me go. My family must come first though. I loved them and would not do anything to endanger them. It had to stop. It occurred to me that the phone calls and the visions had frightened me at times, but I had never considered my family's safety or my own. I questioned my priorities and with that resolve, I went to bed and slept undisturbed for the first time in weeks.

* * * *

Two weeks later I unlocked the front door of my house, stepped into the foyer and froze. I did not see anyone, but I knew that someone had been in my house. I stood still, unaware that I was holding my breath, and surveyed all that I could see from the entrance. My thoughts were scattered; did I run back to the car or did I walk into my house? I would not let whoever had been there frighten me. My stubbornness shielded the fear, and I crept slowly through each room, my eyes wide darting back and forth, searching for the intruders. Heart pounding anxiety made me shiver with each step. When I reached the kitchen, I abruptly stopped. Everything in the room was in disarray. Startled by a noise I screamed, and then realized it was only the phone ringing. I picked up the receiver saying nothing and again heard the soft female voice.

"They're watching you. Stop!"

CHAPTER TWELVE

Deeper into the woods the pickup truck traveled. Sheri listened carefully to the sounds beneath the truck struggling to recognize something, anything that might tell her where they were taking her. Tape over her eyes had once again reduced her to darkness and the fear that comes with a loss of sight.

Sheri heard the constant *ka-thump, ka-thump* of the grooves in the pavement, and a distant, wailing train whistle. She almost tumbled into the floor as the pickup truck ricocheted over a set of rough railroad tracks. She tried to count the turns, but her blinded state altered her balance and made it difficult for her to determine whether the truck veered right or left. She heard gravel hitting the underside of the pickup and she felt the roughness of the road. The bearded man had not reduced the truck's speed as he turned off onto the graveled road, and the pickup slid sideways several times causing Sheri's head to hit the dash.

When they finally stopped the bearded man jerked Sheri out of the truck and dragged her through the woods; briars and undergrowth tearing at her skin. Dazed and unable to see she stumbled on the ground several times before she was thrown into an old, plank, hunting shack. The bearded man removed the tape from her eyes with a jerk, not caring that he tore out her lashes and brows.

"Did you kill her?"

Sheri heard the voice, opened her stinging eyes and saw the sandy-haired man staring into her face. Beside him stood the young woman she had seen before at the vacant house.

Most of the shack's broken windows were covered with flattened, cardboard boxes shoved into the openings. Only a small stream of sunlight filtered through the holes in the roof where the rust had eaten away the tin. Sheri's eyes adjusted to the dimness as she looked around trying to determine where she was. The shack was repulsive, filled with the stench of mold and dope, old, rotting mattresses covered most of the floor, and liquor bottles were piled high in a corner. Spider webs hung from the ceiling and clung to the walls.

She was left alone, gagged and tied, with only an occasional warden bringing food and water. She knew she was being watched; she felt their eyes. She sat in the corner completely unaware of time, waiting for her destiny to unfold. Why wouldn't they let her go now that she was in the woods and the ransom paid? She did not understand their reason for holding her if money was their motive. No tears were left. The unbearable fear was gone. Hopelessness had somehow replaced them. She watched a spider building an intricate web glistening in the filtered stream of sunlight.

Sheri could think of nothing but her family. She knew they were searching for her and would continue to do so. Her dad was like a bloodhound and he would leave nothing untouched. She wistfully smiled at the mental image. She wished that she had called her mother before leaving Grammy's house. That strange and frightful day seemed decades ago. She wondered if she had not gone to Grammy's that day if this kidnapping would have taken place. Her parents must be so frightened for her. She wished she could have spared them this agony because they had given her everything that was important, especially their love. She wondered as she tried to conjure up their loving faces — *will they ever know how much I loved them?*

Her thoughts rambled as she tried to remember how many days she had been gone. *Grammy's ... Grammy's ... Don't go home ... Tell no one ... You're in great danger, child.* The overheard conversation at the party. That's why she was abducted. Whoever they were, they would not let her live. *You should have kept your mouth shut, lady.*

Sheri knew there was nothing she could do to help herself. She sighed, but still there were no tears. She thought about Larry and how she had told him of the overheard conversation at the party. She had not heard them specifically mention drug trafficking, but what else could it have been? Trucks, escorts and millions of dollars? She finally realized that Larry was, in part, responsible for her abduction. He had to be — he was the only one she had told besides Grammy. *Why, Larry? Why would you betray me?*

Sheri drifted back to her childhood as she mindfully watched the spider building its web. There was comfort in those memories and she needed to be comforted. She thought about her grandparents and those wonderful cookies. Funny, she had not thought about her grandmother's homemade cookies in years. And why after all these years, did thoughts of her grandmother's neighbor keep surfacing especially now? She could close her eyes and see the neighbor's face, her laughing, sea green eyes and she felt a strange peace. She did not understand any of this, but it really did not matter now. She heard the savage voices outside and knew she would never go home. "Let's git her out here, now!"

"Come on, bitch, it's time to have some, what I call fun!" sneered the bearded man as he pulled her across the rough, plank floor out into the woods, through the briars and underbrush. He shoved the side of her face down onto the reeking ground causing blood to pour like a spout from her mouth as her teeth cut through her lips.

Sheri saw his dead, cold eyes staring at her through pieces of his stringy hair. He licked his lips drooling brown spittle down the corners of his mouth, and spit tobacco juice on the ground beside her. His cheap cologne reeked of musk, and it made her stomach churn. She felt his sweaty, calloused hands on her skin when he jerked her shirt over her head.

Sheri watched as though she was someone else, somewhere else. Not this person in this place. The sandy-haired man pulled off his shirt, exposing layers of stomach fat bulging over his belt. She heard the sound of a zipper as its metal teeth separated, and the clanging of his belt buckle. She heard the woman curse them. Whimpers escaped from beneath Sheri's gag while the men tore at her flesh, thrusting themselves into her, one after the other. She lay helpless, no fight, no prayers. Welcomed blackness swept over her in uncontrollable waves.

The bearded man's girlfriend, Karen watched while the men brutally raped Sheri. She was appalled and had screamed for them to stop. Sheri did not deserve this kind of treatment. No woman did. Karen was tough and emotionally hard, conditioned by the life she lived, but she was not so hardened that her feelings were completely dead. She looked at Sheri's battered, bruised body lying on the ground and knew that she must do something. Karen looked around to see if the two men were watching her, but they were too busy drinking beer and smoking dope to notice anything else. She put Sheri's sweat pants back on her and pulled her shirt over her exposed body.

Karen had wanted to be included in the kidnapping because she needed the money, and it sounded like fun, but she never thought it would come to this. She knew now that her boyfriend had no intentions of letting Sheri go, and she hated him for this evil.

She looked around again to make sure they were not watching her, and sneaked into the shack. On a piece of paper she had found in the midst of the trash on the floor, she hurriedly wrote the names of those responsible. This act of contrition would surely ease her conscience.

As she walked back out of the shack, the bearded man roughly picked Sheri up off the ground and threw her into the bed of the pickup. Karen knew Sheri would be dead in a short time. All she could hope for now was that if someone found Sheri's body, they would also find the note.

"Hold on a minute before you leave. Her gag is not tight enough and you wouldn't want her to start yelling would you?" she asked.

"She couldn't yell if'n she wanted to," said the bearded man, laughing. "She's had so much fun she's all tuckered out."

"You stupid bastard!" she yelled as she leaned over Sheri and pretended to adjust the gag. She slipped the unseen note she had written into Sheri's pant's pocket, touched her cheek and whispered, "I'm so sorry."

The sandy-haired man climbed into the back of the pickup and the bearded man drove them away. Sheri lay on the floor feeling every jolt of the terrain with her battered body. Her eyes shifted toward the sky and the most breathtaking sunset she had ever seen. It was as if the heavens were welcoming her, painting the sky with a palette of hues no one ever had been privileged to see. Sheri wanted to hold the beauty in her mind until the very end.

They traveled only a short distance before stopping, and she was jerked out of the truck and pulled across the muddy ground. The bearded man kicked her in the side, and as he did, Sheri noticed that his boots had expensive gold metal tips on the toes. She was acutely aware of her surroundings even though she was writhing in pain, and she thought that was odd. She saw decaying trees lying on the ground around her, apparently an old timber site. She noticed a tall radio tower, its lights barely visible in her peripheral vision. She heard water gently slapping a shore somewhere in the distance. She was on her back in the mud looking directly up the muzzle of a pistol.

Remember this. I must remember every detail — the surroundings, the bearded man, the shack, the sounds. Can anyone help me now? Can anyone hear me? Oh, dear God, make this be over quickly!

Sheri forced her mind to concentrate and a tremendous calm overcame her. She became extremely light-headed and suddenly felt as though she was floating, as if she was no longer a part of her own body, the one that was lying on the ground. She wondered if she was already dead.

"You should 'a kept your mouth shut, lady. They don't like

smart-ass busybodies. You could 'a ruined the whole operation if'n you'd told anybody else. Good damn thing you told your old man so he could warn the bosses," the bearded man growled.

Sheri lay there looking up at the pistol while the bearded man kicked her again and again snarling obscenities. The sandy-haired man nervously looked around making sure no one was watching.

She thought of the people she loved. She saw their faces. Her dad, her mother, her sister, her grandparents and even her dog, and once again her grandmother's neighbor. Sheri saw herself as a child running across her grandmother's kitchen to hug this woman. She heard a sound like a firecracker, and slowly inhaled as the bullet left its chamber.

With quiet determination she looked into the face of her killer, seeing instead, the face of her husband.

"I forgive you," she whispered. Her eyes closed as a single tear slid down her cheek.

CHAPTER THIRTEEN

Reports dominated the news with updates on the investigation of Sheri Noland's kidnapping. Her family knew in their hearts that she had passed on, yet they continued to hope and pray. The Hilliards had gone home to Madison, Tennessee, Beth had returned to the university and life continued in spite of tragedy, but for this family it would be forever altered.

Christmas came and went, but Sheri was not forgotten. Eminent magazines featured interviews with Sheri's parents, their grieving faces displayed on the cover. Her father hired investigators who searched around the clock, exploring every possible lead. Wayne Hilliard knew there were others involved in his daughter's abduction. He knew in the depth of his being that Ann Weisman and Daniel Spicer had not acted alone. If only he could piece together the puzzle that had heaped destruction upon his family.

He had questions but could get no answers. Why were the FBI and local authorities so quick to dispel solid evidence or refuse to investigate leads? Why were there no tape recordings of Sheri's final telephone calls to Larry? He knew the calls were recorded. He had personally watched the procedure. According to the FBI the recording equipment malfunctioned on those particular calls, but they retained tapes of the other calls. Something was not right and he knew it. He vowed he would find the others involved if it took everything he owned and the remainder of his life.

* * * *

Michael Runyan had been senior partner in the firm of Wise, Runyan & Queen for as long as most of the employees could remember.

A quiet man of forty-eight who looked ten years older, he had a reputation for occasional losses of memory, bouts of exaggerated anger, and a peculiar way of doing things unlike anyone else in the firm. Otherwise, he was always the Southern gentleman. Still, many of the associates, especially the younger ones, kept their distance. They assumed correctly that Runyan wished it so.

Larry Noland shifted in his chair outside Runyan's office. It was Monday morning and he had been directed to the senior partner's secretary as soon as he entered the building. It was ten minutes past six. He had bypassed his own office and was still holding his top-coat and briefcase in his lap. Runyan never met with associates in the office unexpectedly and Noland was anxious. The secretary's phone buzzed and she lifted the receiver to her heavily painted face.

"Yes sir," she mumbled and then turned to Larry. "They'll see you now. You can leave your things behind my desk."

Larry rose, summoned all the confidence he could muster, and walked through the door into Michael Runyan's office. Runyan rose, as did David Queen, another partner and Congressman Wise.

"Larry." Runyan was a pro at Southern gentility and his voice was appropriately enthusiastic. "I'm so pleased you could make it this early. Please, do sit down."

Larry shook the outstretched hands of the two partners and Con-gressman Wise and sat, not before they did, in a single chair facing the large mahogany desk. Runyan's demeanor shifted and he spoke in quieter tones.

"First of all let me say again that I am so sorry about our little Sheri. I suppose there's still no word?"

"Thank you," Larry responded humbly. "And no, we don't know anything else at this point."

"Well, it must be just horrible for you." Runyan was now taking on the role of comforting father figure, a role as awkwardly por-trayed as it was felt. "If there's anything the firm can do ..."

There was an awkward pause. Congressman Wise and David

Queen exchanged anxious glances.

Runyan continued, "You know Larry, it's not been that long. If you feel you need more time, if you're not ready to be back at work I'm sure something could be arranged."

"No sir. I'm quite ready to be working again. There's nothing more for me to do at home, and I feel that staying busy is the best thing for me right now. I can't just sit around indefinitely." He hoped he had not come across as being too indifferent to his tragedy.

Runyan smiled. It was a frustrated smile and Larry knew it. He amended his answer. "But then, I might find that I could work better at home."

"Oh no, no, no," Runyan interjected. "If you think you're ready to be back then we want you back. It's just that we didn't want you to feel any pressure. We're here to work with you. We're a family here and just want what's best for you, son."

"I feel it's best that I get back on track with work."

"Well, then," Runyan said as he smiled again, "Welcome back." He stood, extended his hand which Larry dutifully shook, and added, "remember, if there's anything we can do ..."

"Thank you, sir." Larry shook the hand of the other partner and the congressman and left the room, closing the door behind him. It struck him odd that the partners would call him in at six in the morning just to be certain he was ready to return to work.

Runyan turned in his seat to the congressman. "Let's handle this, but let's be subtle about it."

Congressman Wise nodded and he and David Queen left the room. Runyan picked up his phone and dialed.

"Hello, Bob? This is Michael Runyan up here in Canton. How are you? Fine, just fine. Listen Bob, I was wondering if I could get some help from you. You know call in that favor you owe me? It may be a few weeks, but I've got a young associate here — he's sharp as a tack, and he wants to relocate to Atlanta. Do you understand? Good. I think he may need a little coaxing. Do you think there could be a place for him in your firm? Why, yes, he'd come not only with my personal recommendation, but the Congressman's as well. He's a fine defense attorney, and I know your firm could always use a fine defense attorney. Well good, we'll send whatever you need. Thank you. Oh and Bob, his name is Larry Noland. Is that going to be a problem? I didn't think so. Good. You'll keep an eye on him now. Won't you? You give my best to that lovely wife of yours. Fine. Good-bye."

He pressed the intercom line on his phone and dialed the number for Personnel. "Hello, Beverly, this is Michael Runyan. I need you to pull a file for me and send it to Atlanta."

* * * *

Within a month, Larry Noland had placed his house on the market for a quick sale and was on his way to Atlanta to the firm of England, Nollig, McBride & Selten, P.C. He had clerked at this firm a few years earlier and was offered a job there after he passed the bar exam, but Congressman Wise thought it a better choice for Larry to join his firm in Canton. They were a close-knit group and shared a certain kind of loyalty not found in larger firms, but it was time for Larry to leave the small town. The firm could not afford further gossip or suspicion connected to Larry. He was creating problems for them.

CHAPTER FOURTEEN

Sarah Hilliard accompanied by her sister and younger daughter, Beth sat motionless in a house once filled with the spirit of youth, Sheri's house. On the kitchen counter in an unopened envelope postmarked three weeks earlier, were the results of Sheri's bar exam. Sarah opened the envelope and smiled. Her daughter had passed on the first attempt. How pleased she would have been had she known. Sarah held tightly onto the piece of paper but with no conscious thought of it in her hand. She had walked through every room of the house longing for her daughter as she examined its contents.

Sheri had been missing more than three months without a trace, and although no one except Larry seemed able to accept Sheri's death as a reality, it was time to try to put the past in order. Sarah would never relinquish hope, but there were things that needed to be done. Larry had a potential buyer for the house in preparation for his move to Atlanta, and he wanted Sheri's belongings removed, things he did not want.

Sarah removed the photographs from their places on shelves and tables, and sighed as memories of her first born flooded her mind. There were photographs of Sheri and her younger sister grinning lopsided for the camera, Sheri and her college friends trying to be serious and astute. Absently she walked away from the photographs and into the master bedroom. Sarah stood in the middle of the room, her eyes devoid of recognition, staring at the walls as if she did not know what to do next. She treaded softly on the lush carpet to the closet and with hesitation opened the doors. Choking back the pain, she touched Sheri's clothes hanging in the closets, the scent of her perfume lingering. Sarah buried her face in one of

Sheri's blouses and caressed it as though she were soothing her daughter.

She felt considerable guilt violating her daughter's privacy, but she continued with the task, knowing Sheri would have wanted her to do this. She witnessed a familiar clutter of news clippings, yearbooks, and an assortment of objects that held the whole of her daughter's history. As she shuffled through them she forgot for a moment that Sheri was gone.

Sarah remembered the lavish wedding gifts, many of them still secure in boxes stored away until needed. Sheri and Larry had received so many gifts from close friends, but Larry did not want or need any of these household items. It was as though he wanted no reminders of his and Sheri's life together, and that thought brought greater sadness to Sarah. The china passed down from Sheri's grandmother should have commanded its rightful place beside the beautiful silver pieces in the china cabinet, but all of it was gone. Realizing that many of her daughter's heirloom pieces were missing, and all that remained in the house were furniture pieces from Sheri's law school apartment, her clothes, pictures and personal items devastated her. Someone had removed everything of value. Larry had not mentioned to her that anything was removed so she searched the house again, and her anger escalated momentarily replacing her grief.

In an effort to calm her mother, Beth called Larry to ask about the missing items.

"My mother took everything of value out of the house because she didn't want anything to be stolen since I was not there," Larry said. "She donated the silver to her church. She thought Sheri would have wanted that."

Beth's anger now surpassed her mother's. "Where is the china that my grandmother gave Sheri?" she yelled, her hand shaking wildly in the air.

"My mother has that at her house. I'm sure she would consider selling it to Ms. Hilliard if she wants it," Larry said. "But she would need to discuss that with my mother. I don't care what happens to the stuff."

Unable to comprehend the maliciousness of this act, Beth vehemently expressed her thoughts to Larry before hanging up the phone, and then returned her attention to her mother. They would confront Katherine Noland another time because she would not allow this horrible woman to add more pain to an already unbearable day. Finally calmed after the emotional upheaval caused by Larry and his mother, Sarah now sat in the kitchen staring through dull, grief-stricken eyes at the profound emptiness that surrounded her. Still and lifeless the house no longer possessed a soul, its heartbeat forever silenced, its light extinguished.

Sarah Hilliard began with the day Sheri was born and relived memories of her precious daughter as she held onto the piece of paper. Sheri taking her first steps, saying mama and dada as she lay cuddled in Sarah's arms, Sheri's excitement over her new baby sister, her first day at school. The sheer happiness on Sheri's face when she saw her daddy coming home from work, then Sheri in high school and college. She saw Sheri's tears as she held and consoled her over yet another argument with her future husband, law school, the wedding. Sheri's beautiful smile as she waved goodbye and left their family cottage in the mountains only a week before she was kidnapped. It was the last time Sarah saw her.

She had been strong and determined that she would get through this atrocity, but as she held the vision of her daughter's beautiful face in her mind, the tears began ever so slowly to drop onto her cheeks. Sarah tried but could not stop them, and she began to sob with gut wrenching pain. She knew at that moment she would never survive this loss. She shielded her broken heart with crossed arms and rocked back and forth as though she too would surely die, and not caring if she did.

"My baby ... my baby ... my baby ..."

* * * *

Sheri's father more determined than ever to find his daughter and the people responsible for her kidnapping, continued with a resolve of stone, his pain temporarily replaced with rage. Telephone calls, ten or more per day, flowed into the Hilliard house in a steady stream. Each caller had valuable information to share, but all feared for their lives. They knew there were others involved but could not and would not give him names.

"We have families to protect," one caller proclaimed.

"We know how you must feel but to give you names is a death sentence for us," said another. "Even making this call is risky."

Wayne Hilliard knew the folks of Canton were an unusual breed. They protected each other with a familial bond he could not comprehend. The locals knew what went on there, but they would not speak of it. Those who held the power and money controlled the town and Wayne knew if you were born and raised there, you stayed there. They might physically leave the town but they were always connected to the people there in one way or another. He knew all this, he had seen it first hand, but he could not understand it. It was a small, Southern town loyalty that made no sense to him. The locals did not like outsiders and they trusted no one. Almost anyone could be bought for the right price, and if you could not be, you disappeared plain and simple. That was their life.

"You should check out the area around Gilmer County," another caller said with an extreme Southern drawl. He spoke of mountains and caves in the area claiming to know the other people involved. "Be very careful when you go there. They're watching you," he continued. "They got rid of Daniel Spicer before he could talk, didn't they? You're in our prayers."

Wayne Hilliard enlisted the help of several out-of-state psychics renowned for their expertise in solving crimes for the FBI. All of them saw water, saw others involved, saw the bearded man with layers of gold around his neck, but none of them could tell him Sheri's whereabouts, and the search continued.

CHAPTER FIFTEEN

Arriving late again, I charged into the break room for coffee passing by the group of secretaries and paralegals huddled around the coffeepot who were discussing the newest addition to the firm.

"Did you know that he's the husband of that kidnapped woman?" one of the older ladies said, almost whispering.

"Why's he here at our firm?" another asked.

She shook her bleached blond head. "Guess he couldn't live with all the gossip in Canton."

"He sure moved in a hurry."

"Yeah, it had to be tough on him. Everyone thinks he had something to do with it."

A younger woman with mousy, brown hair frowned slightly. "I don't think he did. How could anyone's husband be a part of something that horrible?"

"I've known husbands who would do anything to get rid of their wives," the older woman said, pouring a cup of coffee. Laughter followed.

"Didn't he clerk here at one time?"

"Yeah, I heard that this firm offered him a job then but he joined the firm in Canton instead," the younger woman said.

Leaving the break room with my coffee, I walked down the stairs, through the atrium and into my office. I noticed nothing except the stack of files on my desk resulting from the distractions of the last few months. My work was piling up fast and I was determined to get caught up. The intercom line on my phone buzzed and I heard the librarian's voice.

"Lynn, hi. Are you real busy this morning?"

"Yes, real. I'm way behind with my work. Why?"

"If you get a chance in the next hour or so, can you come to the library?" she asked. "I need to introduce you to the firm's new associate."

"Sure, if it's really important," I said with a sigh.

"You may need to assist him with trial preparation and it might be a good idea if you got to know him a little before that starts," said the librarian. "The partners are in a hurry to get him working on this case."

"Give me about an hour and I'll see what I can do."

I completed a few more items on my to-do list and walked through the atrium on my way to the library. The newly renovated building was beautiful, and the atrium was an inspiration to all who entered. Lush carpeting and mahogany spiral staircases graced its entrance and produced a feeling of serenity and peace, attributes needed in a hectic law firm.

As I entered the library my senses heightened and an uneasy feeling began to spread down my spine while I searched for the librarian.

"Hi. You needed to see me?"

"Lynn, I'd like you to meet someone." She motioned her head to the table at the end of the corridor.

A young, dark-haired man stood and approached us as the librarian spoke, then extended his hand. "This is Larry Noland. Larry, Lynn Conley."

Larry jerked his hand from mine as though it had been ignited. I could see nothing but black surrounding him, the ebony shade of death, and my throat constricted. We left the library simultaneously — he back to his office, and I out the back door of the building, neither able to speak. The librarian stood with her mouth open in disbelief at the scene she had witnessed, concerned that she had missed an intricate detail somewhere along the way.

What had transpired during that introduction was disturbing. I knew I could not be in the same building with that man, and I could not work with him. Not wanting to go back into the building knowing that he was there, I had to force myself to open the door. I ran back to my office, typed my resignation without submitting it, and left for the day.

Driving home I thought about the strange reaction I had to Larry Noland and vice versa. He did not look sinister, but something was very wrong. I trusted my intuition, but it concerned me even more that he reacted so peculiar. He did not know me and had never met me. There were too many strange occurrences surrounding Sheri Noland's kidnapping.

I thought about the comments heard earlier in the break room. Obviously, I was not the only one with questions about Larry Noland. To what extent was he involved with Sheri's kidnapping?

Over the past several weeks I had continued to search wooded areas around County Road 249. Sometimes Jon went along to ensure my safety and keep me company, but other times I was alone. The answers were hidden there and I was compelled to continue the search in that area.

Taking the long way home, I drove over the foothills using the time to clear my mind. It was cold outside with winter fast approaching and the trees were barren and foreboding against the gray sky. I did not like winter but sometimes it was comforting, like a warm, cozy, flannel blanket snuggled around your shoulders. Across the summit of the next hill I could see my house, and I was anxious to get inside.

Once again I walked into the foyer and felt the hair on the nape of my neck rise. Anger overtook me this time and I screamed out, "Stay out of my house!"

I knew no one could hear me. There was no one there, but it made me feel better. The door had been securely locked when I opened it and nothing looked out of place. I felt no fear as I walked through each room searching for the intruder, only intense anger growing with each step. In the master bathroom another warning — animal feces had been smeared over most of the walls, the floor and the vanities. The remainder of the house was untouched. I screamed again into the silence then changed from my work clothes into sweats and cleaned the bathroom. Exhausted I curled up on the sofa. I was growing wearier with each day's passing. These people were playing a demented game, whoever they were. I had no new information about the kidnapping so why were they doing this?

Jon was out of town and the house was too quiet. I shivered and reached for a blanket pulling it over my legs. While sitting on the sofa thinking about the strange events of the day, the room darkened as though the gray skies had given way to rain. In the darkness once again I saw County Road 249 and concrete tiles, timber sites and Sheri Noland. She was lying motionless on the muddy ground while the bearded man stared at her, the pistol in his hand.

Remember, Lynn do not get emotional. Just be the observer and see what happens. Do not stop the flow of visions, echoed the doctor's words. Trying to remain detached, I watched as the bearded man and the sandy-haired man wrapped Sheri's limp, pale, battered body in a black plastic tarp. They tied a nylon rope around her body securing the tarp wrapping, and then hoisted the bundle up over their shoulders. They began their descent into the woods behind the timber site.

Gone was the darkness and the vision, but I remained on the sofa for a very long time sorting out this nightmare. Contrary to the doctor's advice, I could not remain detached. Sheri had touched my soul and affected me in a way that I would never fully understand. I needed to see this to its end no matter where it took me. Sheri had transcended a realm of the unknown to reach out for help and I heard and felt her cries. I would not abandon her.

* * * *

Larry Noland practically ran back to his office rubbing his hand. Her handshake had burned and that look in her eyes — she knew. Paranoia was settling in, oftentimes a side effect of guilt. She could not possibly know what he had done; no one knew anything except what the FBI and the news media reported, but he had recognized her name. She was that person Detective Little worked with, that psychic who had taken them to the woods. Detective Smith told him all about her and how she saw things. He said she scared the hell out of him because her face got this strange look when she saw something, and her eyes clouded. When she shook his hand today, she wore the look that Smith described. It was eerie. He knew that he would need to be very careful. How would he ever work in the same firm with her, much less work on a case together? He needed to know more about Lynn Conley.

Larry walked into the break room where half a dozen attorneys were reading newspapers and drinking coffee.

"Hi, Stan. How's it going this morning? Find anything interesting in the local gossip section?" he asked one of the attorneys, trying to sound casual. Larry often exaggerated his speech imitating the old Charleston Southern dialect. He knew that it intimidated people in a unique sort of way, and threw them off guard. That charming, slow, Southern drawl also gave him ample time to choose his words with care, and he used it whenever he felt threatened as he did today.

"Oh, nothing interesting today. You know the same crap," Stan said not looking up.

"I read something a couple of days ago that really gave me a laugh," Larry said, trying to get the group's attention without being obvious.

"Yeah, what was that?" questioned another attorney who was listening.

"There was a lengthy article on the crime-solving abilities of psychics," Larry said watching for their reactions as he poured a cup of coffee.

"You know, Larry, I believe in that stuff. I've never seen one in action, but there's documentation that substantiates their ability," said Stan turning back to his coffee.

Another lawyer chimed in. "I think some people actually do have a sixth sense. When I was a kid I had a great-aunt who used to spook me. She could tell you things that would give you nightmares. She had to be a psychic."

"I don't believe any of that shit! People can't see into the future, and they certainly can't pick up vibes from the air!"

"Hey, Larry, what's with the hostility? We're just talking about psychic phenomenon. That stuff's been around forever. Why all this sudden interest? Stan asked raising his eyebrows.

"I just think everyone puts too much value on what these people say. They have no credibility and can't prove anything. Why does anyone even listen to them?"

"The FBI has used psychics for years, and some of them have actually solved crimes. I wouldn't want to meet one unless of course, she was blond and beautiful. Oh, and could give me tips on the stock market before I invested," Stan said. Laughter broke out in the room as subtle lascivious comments were thrown around.

"You just get up on the wrong side of the bed this morning, Larry?" asked another attorney.

Larry shook his head, threw up his hand and walked out of the break room with thoughts running rampant. He needed to get out of the city for a while and calm himself before he did something else stupid. What must his colleagues think of his behavior? It's her fault. She caused this outburst, the bitch psychic that burned his hand. Fear, that's what he felt, scared-to-death crazy fear. He had to go and go now, go to the beach away from those idiot FBI agents who were still watching him. He was sick of it, sick of them.

He left that afternoon to spend a couple of days at Sea Island. Walking on the beach and feeling the breeze off the water always made him feel better. He had been there many times before but not with his wife. Memories of those days and nights, but especially the nights were a welcome diversion. He rested, ate in expensive restaurants and browsed in shops. No one was watching him. He could do as he pleased and enjoy the days away from the city and away from the prying eyes, but he knew he had to go back. There was no way to run from the others. He had done exactly as he had been told, so why didn't they leave him alone? Why didn't everyone leave him alone?

Larry sat on the balcony of his hotel overlooking the ocean and thought about the gossip saturating Canton, always directed at him as though he was some kind of two-headed monster. People expected him to display his grief according to their standards, and when he did not, they assumed he was hiding something. He was filled with grief as any husband should be over losing his wife, but he did not feel he should be required to justify his behavior to anyone except the firm.

Michael Runyan had admonished him because he drank a little too much beer at the football game and someone overheard him refer to his missing wife as a spoiled bitch. So what? She was and he was glad she was dead, even though he should not have said so.

He did not understand why the partners in Canton were so eager to send him to Atlanta. He had done what they asked of him and still they wanted to be rid of him. Well, it was their loss. He was a great lawyer and an asset to any firm. Congressman Wise even suggested that he should have spent more time participating in the organized searches for Sheri because the media exposure was important, he said, and people expected to see the husband desperately searching for his wife. What a crock of shit! Let the ones who cared go searching, like her parents. It made them feel necessary.

He had loved Sheri from the first moment he saw her, but as the years passed she became dull and boring. She was a spoiled daddy's girl and Larry knew she would never grow with him. She did not rise to the occasion when it was necessary, and he just could not accept that from his wife. His career, powerful colleagues and social status were important, and Sheri did not seem to care about any of those things. She cared about stupid issues like sick or abused children, world hunger and social injustices for God's sake. Why would anyone care about insignificant problems such as those?

He could not understand her, and she always compared him to her father which raised his hackles. He knew he was smarter than his father-in-law, and definitely smarter than Sheri. He was capable of taking care of his wife, his way, and he had not needed anyone to tell him otherwise.

Larry knew that if he kept his mouth shut and was an obedient servant to Congressman Wise and the partners he would lack for nothing, but his temper got the best of him, and he seemed to overreact at the worst possible times. He needed to work on that, but all things considered, he was doing the best he could.

He did not want to return to Atlanta but he had no choice. The third scotch in less than an hour was beginning to affect his mood, and as he continued to sit on the balcony staring at the water, unwanted thoughts racked his mind.

It was purely accidental the day his life changed directions. Michael Runyan's office door was open and inviting, the room vacant. Passing by on his way to the conference room, Larry was unable to resist getting a closer look at the senior partner's lush office. He walked inside closing the door behind him, breathing in the affluence permeating the air. *Now, this is what being a lawyer is all about*, he thought.

Larry ran his hand over the distressed, expensive, leather sofa admiring its exquisite beauty, and then unable to stop himself, sat down on the designer chair behind the polished desk. Currents of power surged through his veins as he envisioned himself the commander of the hierarchy in the firm.

Lost in his fantasy, he unlocked the desk and began opening the drawers rummaging through the contents of hidden files. One in particular caught his attention. He placed it on the desk, opened it and began to read. Unaware of time or the fact that he was trespassing, he continued to absorb the information contained in the file astonished at his findings.

Michael Runyan entered his office so quickly that Larry had no time to react, the file still open in his hands.

"Well, well, well, now son, just what do we have here? You do understand the seriousness of your actions, I presume?" Runyan said with deadly quiet authority. "May I have the file you are so intensely perusing?"

Larry handed the file over to his boss and removed himself from behind Runyan's desk waiting for his wrath to spark. The senior partner swallowed hard when he realized which file Larry was reading.

"You see yourself filling my shoes someday. Do you? We all strive to do what's right in this world, son, and doing the right thing is what makes this firm a family. You understand don't you? We each have an important role to play in the scheme of things, and we are all justly rewarded."

Runyan never took his eyes off Larry as though casting a hypnotic spell upon him. Noland could say nothing. He was bound by legal ethics regarding what he read and Michael Runyan's threat seeped into his brain. He had just become an active member of this family through error, but the rules were very clear. Should he break them, well, he did not want to entertain that option.

* * * *

"Enough of this reminiscing," Larry said out loud. He was not compelled to look back. He gulped down the remains of his scotch, looked out at the ocean once more and returned to his room to pack.

The drive back to Atlanta filled Larry with a new resolve, one of determination and to hell with the FBI. He was protected and they could not touch him.

He cranked up the music and his car reverberated with the sound of his laughter.

CHAPTER SIXTEEN

"Court is now in session all rise," commanded the bailiff.

"Case number CA93-4581 is a Presumption of Death action brought by the petitioner, Larry Noland, Jr., to determine the legal death of his wife, Sheridan Hilliard Noland. I understand that Mrs. Noland has been missing for over two years and her body has not been recovered. Is that correct?"

"Yes, Your Honor, that is correct. My client, Mr. Larry Noland with great sadness has petitioned this court to declare her legally dead, God rest her soul," stated Bob Selten of England, Nollig, McBride & Selten.

"I'm sorry, Mr. Noland. I see we have a couple of Motions in Opposition to this Petition. I'll hear the State's objection first and then we'll move on with the insurance company's, so let's get started," instructed the judge.

"Thank you, Your Honor," the state attorney respectfully replied.

"The state objects to Mr. Noland's Petition on the grounds of Georgia Code § 53-9-1. The four-year death statute has not been met. The statute clearly states that a person of this state who has been missing from the last known place of domicile for a continuous period of four years shall be presumed to have died; provided, however, that such presumption of death may be rebutted by proof." The state attorney continued.

"It has only been two years since Mrs. Noland was kidnapped, and the state does not feel that is sufficient time to declare her dead considering the suspicious circumstances surrounding her abduction." His eyes darted toward Larry with contempt. The FBI's case was procedurally open although not actively being investigated.

Walker's Insurance Company proceeded next with its objection based on suspicious circumstances surrounding the victim's disappearance, and the fact that a body had not been recovered. Therefore, death had not been sufficiently proven pursuant to Georgia Code.

"Your Honor, my client would like to wrap up all the loose ends of this sensitive matter," Bob Selten addressed the court. "Mrs. Noland had several trust accounts; the residential property in Canton needs to be disposed of. Then, Your Honor, there's the matter of the life insurance policy, and there were many investments. Until the court declares her legally dead, God rest her soul, all of these matters are at a standstill."

"Mr. Hilliard, do you and Mrs. Hilliard have any objections to Mr. Noland's Petition that is before this Court to have your daughter declared legally dead?" asked the judge as a courtesy to the parents.

"Your Honor, we feel that it is too soon, but considering the fact that there is a substantial sum of money involved and Sheri has been missing for more than two years, we do need to move forward. The trusts that were set up in Sheri's name individually must be transferred, and the residential property held jointly should be released. Larry has a potential buyer for the residence, and I know of no other way to accomplish this," said the Hilliard's lawyer.

"The state's motion and Walker's motion is duly noted for the record and we will proceed accordingly," stated the judge as he studied the Petition.

Hours passed while Larry's attorney and Sheri's parents and their attorney worked out the details of the Petition. The residential property was released to Larry so that he could finalize the pending sale. The trusts and all other accounts held in Sheri's name individually would be transferred to the Hilliard's younger daughter, Beth. The life insurance was held in abeyance pending the final outcome of the FBI investigation. The policy entitlement would not be paid to Larry until the four-year statute was met, or Sheri's body recovered, whichever came first. The judge declared Sheridan Hilliard Noland legally deceased effective that day by granting Larry Noland's Petition.

Larry and his attorney left the courtroom slightly distressed. Larry had hoped for more, but considering Mr. Hilliard's insistence that the trusts and investments he had set up for Sheri were only for Sheri's benefit, Larry was not entitled to any of it. He was angry over the life insurance policy because he was entitled to payment as the beneficiary, and he did not think he should have to wait another two years to receive it. The policy was large and he wanted the cash.

Larry had no intentions of placing his life on hold because he had plans, big plans. He stopped in the courthouse corridor by the pay phones on his way out and made a call. "It's over, baby. Now we can get on with our lives. I'm a legally free man," Larry whispered.

The purring, eager voice on the other end of the phone line belonged to a young woman Larry had met several years ago. They clerked at the same firm and attended law school together. She was well connected descending from an established law family with old money, and she would be an excellent boost to his career. Larry was eager to move on with his plans and put the past where it belonged — dead.

The others had encouraged him to make this move insisting that it would benefit all of them in time. Bob Selten insisted that the Presumption of Death Petition be filed. There was no reason to wait the four years and he knew the judge would grant the petition to repay a few favors the firm had extended him.

Bob Selten also knew from experience that Larry needed to establish a new life, one that would eliminate the gossip. As long as Larry remained under suspicion he brought bad publicity to the firm. With the influence of the future Mrs. Noland's family, Larry and the firm would once again retain their good standing.

Congressman Wise and Bob Selten had shared political ties for many years. Bob, previously a state legislator, had helped the Congressman obtain his position. They worked well together through a network of affluent and well connected people in several states, and they disguised their various acquisitions through political channels. The firm with their help, had accomplished great things, but they simply were not prepared for the chaos created by Sheri Noland's botched kidnapping. Mr. Hilliard would not stop his obsessive investigation, and something had to be done. The Congressman and selected partners of both firms had been very meticulous accomplishing their plans. Great measures were taken to ensure that Daniel Spicer and Ann Weisman would be the only ones accused of the kidnapping. All the loose ends were tied up — except Wayne Hilliard. He could jeopardize all they had worked for if he was allowed to continue with his investigation. Not one of them thought that after two years he would still be searching for his daughter. They had greatly underestimated him.

* * * *

The trucking company was a brilliant decision. A bonus. Clients you could count on. They could transport the profitable white powder undetected anywhere in the United States. The escorts were ever present and well disguised. Most of the drivers were unaware that they were hauling anything other than the items listed on their manifests. The compartments were so well concealed in the trailers that even the Department of Transportation inspectors could not find them.

Partners of three law firms, their political associates, a few judges, many business executives and particularly the syndicate, were profiting hundreds of millions of dollars, and they would let no one stand in their way, much less someone like Wayne Hilliard. The enlistment of selected state and federal officials would insure their continued prosperity. The list included, but was not limited to, select FBI agents, police officers and deputies, the district attorney, and the sitting governor. Whatever they needed or wanted they received with no questions asked. Their financial backing was immeasurable. The organized crime syndicate met their every need.

* * * *

Wayne Hilliard received an anonymous, untraceable phone call giving him information about a young woman who had placed a note in Sheri's pocket containing the names of those responsible for Sheri's kidnapping and subsequent death. The young woman, according to the source, was present at a shack in the woods where Sheri was held captive. Unable to keep this information to herself, the young woman had told certain members of her family about her act of contrition, but never divulged the names on the note. She was identified only by her first name, Karen.

The others would have no impropriety in their tightly knit group. They promptly ordered the disposal of the young woman after learning about the phone call to Hilliard. The Canton police found her body several days later wrapped in a black tarp, floating on a lake. Her alleged killer was arrested and sentenced, and having a voluminous rap sheet guaranteed due process. Ann Weisman had also been silenced by signing a confession and sentenced to life in prison without parole, and all accomplished without a trial. She was safely tucked away and no one could get to her without first going through Michael Runyan, her attorney, and he allowed no one to visit her. Daniel Spicer was dead. The next step was to keep Mr. Hilliard from continuing his investigation.

* * * *

One month later as darkness approached, the newly renovated building with its beautiful atrium emptied, a private conference ensued. Sitting around the mahogany table in a beautifully decorated conference room, the local masterminds planned their next and final step with respect to Sheri Hilliard's body.

Bob Selten was a contradiction both in appearance and manner. His always impeccably dressed body bulged at the waist. White hair and bushy eyebrows added an air of distinction to his ruddy complexion and bloated face. His demeanor was coldly polite as soft-spoken words gushed from his mouth. One had the feeling of being face-to-face with a deadly viper when in his presence. He accepted nothing less than perfection from his associates and legal assistants, but he was disorganized with his own cases. His luxuriously decorated office was cold and impersonal, its furnishing stiff and formal. No family photos or personal items were placed in his office, and clients' case files were scattered over the floor.

Respected but also feared, Bob Selten had called this meeting because he intended to get rid of Wayne Hilliard's snooping once and for all. Seated around the conference table were Michael Runyan, David Queen, Congressman Wise, District Attorney Donald Butcher, the elder Noland, and Judge Henry Johnson.

"Gentlemen, I'm so glad you all could make it," he began. "Well now, let's get started. First of all, let me say that I'm pleased we are all doing so well with our little venture. But we seem to have run into a little snag along the way, and we need to remove it." He cleared his throat, took a drink of water and continued.

"Let's send our good friend, Mr. Wayne Hilliard, a message that there is a new witness in his daughter's case and that said witness is willing to talk. A bit like turning the fox loose in the henhouse wouldn't you say? He'll go right after the bait."

The others nodded affirmatively.

"Certainly sounds workable to me. What are you proposing?" Michael Runyan said with a chuckle.

"You remember that young girl, Karen, who put the note in our little Sheri's pocket? Her killer is serving a life sentence for murder and is out of the way, but his family needs help. And we all know how important family is, don't we?" The others at the table nodded in agreement.

"Well now," he continued. "We could arrange a little gift, say for instance, pay off the gambling debts, give them a little spending money, and maybe look into getting him a reduced sentence. He would have no choice but to help us with this little mission," Selten proclaimed, quite proud of his brilliance as he postured. His years in the legislature had taught him how to be shrewd without a fault.

"He may be one of those cold-hearted killers we read so much about in our newspapers today, but he wouldn't think of crossing us. We just coax him a bit. He'll tell Hilliard where he put the body and that he was helping Daniel Spicer. Gentlemen, I think the Lake Lanier area would work quite well. It's about fifty miles away and aren't there caves just northeast of that area?" he asked, smiling.

"Splendid! What does he have to lose?" Donald Butcher interjected. "We know they will never find the body. Even after he confesses to Hilliard he won't be convicted of this alleged crime."

"Exactly. Mr. Hilliard then pursues the search for his little girl's body in that area and he's out of our hair for good. He'll stop this insidious investigation here if he has knowledge of the body's alleged location there.

"How long will it take to implement this plan?" asked Congressman Wise.

"About as long as it takes to place this call." Bob Selten picked up the phone.

CHAPTER SEVENTEEN

I slept but it was a disturbed slumber. A ghost was chasing me and fear paralyzed my every move. I awoke tugging at the sheets, perspiration dripping from my face. The voice whispered, "Call my daddy. Call my daddy if you don't want to get hurt."

I recognized the voice, the same one that told me to go north only weeks before when I doubted my sanity. Why didn't she leave me alone? What could I possibly do to help her? I looked at the clock, and with disgust realized it was six thirty in the morning. I could not go back to sleep now, so I stumbled to the kitchen and poured a cup of coffee as Jon walked in and turned on the light.

"What are you doing up at this hour when you're not even working?" His teasing stopped when he saw the look on my face. "What's wrong?"

"I had a nightmare; ghosts were chasing me. That voice kept telling me to call her daddy," I said squinting against the light.

"What voice?" John looked concerned now as he sat down next to me.

"The one that told me to go north a few weeks ago. Remember, I thought I was hearing things."

He placed his hand gently on my arm. "I'm really concerned about you. You're not sleeping again; you're hearing voices, now you're up at dawn. What happened to the person who could sleep until noon?" He narrowed his eyes as if to get a better look into the mysteries of my mind.

"Do you think she meant literally to call her dad?" I asked.

"Who knows? You're the weird one in this family. I don't hear voices and I don't see what's not there like you," Jon said laughing.

"Maybe you should call him. I'm not sure how you would tell him about these visions, but it couldn't hurt. He may just think you're strange like I do."

He grinned that little boy grin that always made me laugh, and walked out on the veranda still talking. "Then he can worry about this instead of you."

What would I do without Jon? He kept me from being too serious because he always found humor in the worst of things. He had been my strength since the beginning. I knew I frightened him with these visions, although this was not his first experience with them. Sometimes they frightened me and I should be accustomed to them after all the years, but the visions of Sheri Noland were different from the others. I felt these visions as though I was re-living the events. And the voices? Any mental expert would diagnose that as possible schizophrenia. I poured another cup of coffee and stared into its black velvet darkness.

Jon had resigned himself to the fact that I could not make the visions go away. I promised him that I would be careful and not involve our family in any way, but I had not told him about the bathroom and the smeared animal feces yet. He was already far too worried about me because he knew how stubborn I could be. I would not allow my family to be hurt, but I had to continue trying to help Sheri Noland. She gave me no choice.

I waited until nine that morning and began trying to locate a phone number for Sheri's father, which I thought I could get from the minister of the church responsible for organizing the search parties. After several attempts I was given the number and I called his office.

"Mr. Hilliard, this is Lynn Conley. You and I have never met and I'm not sure that I have a right to call you, but ..." I paused and took a deep breath. "I have information that I would like to share with you about your daughter. Can we meet somewhere? I don't feel comfortable discussing this on the phone."

"Where are you calling from?" Mr. Hilliard asked.

"Atlanta," I said.

"Can you meet me tonight at a restaurant around six o'clock? It will take me a few hours to get there."

"Yes, I can meet you. Just tell me where."

"Do you mind if I bring my lawyer? He needs to be included in this discussion."

"No, I don't mind at all," I said.

We agreed on the restaurant and I spent the day wondering how I would ever tell him what I had seen and heard. I had nothing concrete to validate my information, and if I were Mr. Hilliard, I would certainly want something more than an account of strange visions from a person I did not know. The afternoon slipped into evening and I asked God for guidance as I drove to the meeting.

We each had given the other a description of our cars, and Mr. Hilliard and his lawyer were waiting for me as I drove into the parking lot. Looking around I hurried to the restaurant door stopping only long enough to shake hands and exchange introductions before entering. Mr. Hilliard was a soft-spoken, pleasant, humble man on the surface, but underneath I could feel the currents of his wrath and pain. Although shrouded in anguish, his face was strong and handsome. His strength made me feel protected, but his pain made me want to wrap my arms around him and console him.

The restaurant was noisy and well-meaning servers kept interrupting our conversation. Through many starts and stops, I gave them a narrative of the visions — Sheri's voice giving me directions, and the telephone calls received from the proclaimed judge.

As though he was preparing for a trial, the lawyer wrote page upon page of notes detailing the information I offered. His thick glasses kept sliding down his nose, and he pushed them back in place while nervously rubbing his jaw. Mr. Hilliard wiped tears from his eyes a few times, but retained his composure throughout my recital.

"You've given us invaluable information and we're grateful, Lynn," Mr. Hilliard said softly. "I have a couple of out-of-state detectives working on this case and they may want to talk with you. Would that be all right?"

I nodded. "That would be fine, Mr. Hilliard. I'll help in any way possible. I don't know why Sheri chose me, but she's persistent and will not go away." I responded with a grin, hoping a little humor wouldn't offend him.

"She was persistent in life, why wouldn't she be in death as well?" he mused.

We said our goodbyes at the conclusion of our meeting and I left the restaurant. I was tense driving home and could not rid myself of the feeling that I was being watched. I kept checking my rear-view mirror searching the darkness. It was late and I was exhausted after the three-hour meeting. Jon was out of town again and I crept into my too quiet, empty-feeling house, hoping no one had been there. After searching each room, which had become my ritual these days, I climbed into bed, pulling the covers over my head as though I were a child hiding from the scary things of the night.

Several days later I received a phone call from the detectives Mr. Hilliard had spoken about. They wanted to come to my house and discuss the information that I had given Mr. Hilliard and his lawyer. We agreed on the day and time, but they did not ask for directions or my address.

When the doorbell rang I froze even though I knew it was them, and because I was so anxious about the past invasions of my house, I required the detectives to show identification before allowing them in. They were unusual in their appearance but I soon learned they were experts in their field. One of them had long, corn-colored hair pulled back in a ponytail, was dressed in worn, blue jeans, and cowboy boots, and looked like someone right out of a John Wayne Western. He was at least six and a half feet tall and was very thin, and he had to stoop down as he extended his hand to me. He introduced himself as Joe.

The other one, a woman, was more conservative. She was plainly dressed, wore her copper hair short and cropped, and spoke with a Northern accent. She said her name was Vivian and began immediately asking questions. They left nothing untouched or unanswered. Joe produced dozens of photographs and asked if I could identify any of the people in them.

Jon sat on the sofa with a worried look on his face, beginning to fully realize the seriousness of this investigation and my involvement. He walked over to stare out the window several times, uncomfortable with their questioning. I was paralyzed in the chair feeling totally out of my element.

"Lynn, does this look like the gun you saw in the vision?" Joe asked as he pulled a pistol out of his briefcase and handed it to me. I took it reluctantly, uncomfortable with it in my possession. I examined it and nodded yes struggling in unfamiliar territory. I watched their facial expressions as they listened to the narrative of the visions. They glanced at each other with doubtful looks early on, but when our meeting concluded, they were satisfied. I had verified undisclosed information that they had obtained through other sources, and they were astonished at the accuracy.

"We'll be in touch with you, Lynn," they said and walked out the door. Vivian turned back and handed me a piece of paper. "Here's our private phone number and the number of our hotel. Call us if you have any other information."

Jon still had that concerned look on his face as we stood at the door and watched them leave.

"I understand why you met with them today, but I don't understand why you can't let this go now." He shook his head. "I've never seen anything possess you like this case has. I know you want to help but please let the detectives handle this now. They're trained for this work. You're not. I don't want you to get hurt." He placed his arms around me and closed the door shutting out the other world.

* * * *

Several days passed without incident and I felt better about the meeting with the detectives. Now experts had the information from the visions and would act on it. Early evening the phone rang and I expected it to be the detectives.

"Hello?"

"Lynn?" a deep baritone voice asked.

"Yes, this is she," I said not recognizing the voice.

"This is the judge calling."

Shaken by the voice, I took a deep breath before speaking. "I'm happy to finally hear from you rather than your spokesperson. How can I help you?"

"We need to talk. Could you meet me somewhere?"

I clenched my eyes shut and tried to remain calm. "I don't think that's possible. I don't even know who you are."

"You must not continue with this investigation or your search for the dead girl. You're in danger and you must already know that."

He continued almost whispering. "I feel some remorse about this kidnapping and I need to tell you how to protect yourself. You can't and won't implicate me in any way because you're not in a position to do so. I feel confident that you would be most appreciative of the information I'm willing to share with you."

"Why won't you identify yourself by name if you feel so confident that I won't harm you? How do I know you're even a judge?"

"Who I am is not important. What I know is vital, and if you're to come out of this unharmed you need that information. The people involved are powerful and I'm only one small player in their game. They gave me no choice, but you do have a choice. You must meet me somewhere so we can talk."

"I won't meet you, sir. I value my life and although I appreciate the information you've given me, I won't place myself in a situation where I have no control."

I though about his words for a moment and then relented. "If you're sincere then I'll agree to meet with you, but only if I can bring detectives with me to hear your story."

"That's impossible. It must be just you." There was a long pause but he continued. "Maybe you should find out about the party the little Noland girl attended before she was kidnapped. Happened only a few days before. You might find something interesting about the people who attended. I'll at least give you that much."

There was complete silence and then the phone line was dead.

I would recognize the voices of a few federal or state judges because I had been present in their courtrooms for the firm, but I had not heard this voice. Atlanta was a large city with many suburbs, and this man could be a judge anywhere in the area, or possibly not a judge at all. Maybe he would call again. I tried tracing the call through the telephone company, but it was made from a pay phone. I had not thought to turn on a recorder. I did not know whether to be afraid or angry. Why would this man claiming to be a judge call me but refuse to identify himself, and then give me bits and pieces of information before implying a threat? I did not like their game and I did not want to be a part of it.

I waited until the next day to call the detectives. I knew they needed this information to help with their investigation.

"Hi, this is Lynn. I received another call and I need to tell you about it," I said to Vivian on her private line.

"Your phone line may have been compromised and we can't discuss anything. You'll have to call us on the other phone number but not from your house."

I started to ask a question but was interrupted.

"Say nothing. We'll talk later." The detective was insistent.

I called again from a pay phone later in the day. Vivian explained to me that their private phone line, as well as my home phone line, had been tapped and we could have no further discussions on either. Their electronic equipment had detected a signal they knew to be a tap. I was instructed not to discuss anything about this case with anyone on my home phone until the line was cleared.

I recounted the judge's phone conversation and asked the detectives for advice. Vivian informed me that prior to meeting with me, they had asked a renowned psychic from another state to join them the following week for a search. It seemed that this psychic was drawn to an area that had timber sites and concrete drain tiles. They asked if I would be willing to accompany them so we could discuss my visions and the judge's information with the psychic. I agreed to go but the trip never came to fruition.

* * * *

Removed from the case, the detectives were on their way home one week later. When the phone lines were tapped, information they had obtained through anonymous sources was passed on to potentially dangerous people. A deputy with the Sheriff's Department had informed Mr. Hilliard that his detectives were in danger. Although their job placed them in constant jeopardy, Mr. Hilliard was not willing to risk harm to anyone else. The detectives disappeared and the out-of-state psychic's trip was cancelled. The FBI would keep the case open but inactive, and Mr. Hilliard would continue privately with his search, his own way.

CHAPTER EIGHTEEN

Two years had passed since I vowed to do nothing more about Sheri Noland's kidnapping investigation, and the haunting visions that would not let me go. After the detectives were removed from the case, I felt that my continual searching was at an end. If trained professionals could not manage this investigation without endangering lives, I had no place in it. Happy with my life once again, I was employed with a different law firm in Atlanta far away from Larry Noland, and I had no contact with anyone else connected to that atrocity. I wanted to keep it that way forever. My family, job and friends were a comforting, necessary part of my life and I was enjoying them immensely. I had settled into a real life in this city.

My son and daughter had both married just six months apart and begun their own lives. Being included in their happiness increased mine. Their weddings were beautiful, although costly, and my life felt like everyone else's as I reasoned it should be.

I cannot help but wince when people complain because their lives are boring, normal and routine. If only they were allowed to experience the things that surround them and see the mysteries of our universe unfolding, boredom and normal would never be a consideration. I strive to see good in daily life because in the visions so much is ugly. I do not want my world to become tainted because of my gift.

The autumn air was crisp and full of energy on this beautiful Saturday morning as I sat on the veranda overlooking the woods enjoying a glass of iced, raspberry tea. The folded newspaper beside my chair caught my attention. I gasped and almost choked on the tea as I read the headlines on the front page.

JUDGE HENRY JOHNSON FOUND DEAD

ATLANTA, GA. (A.P.) — Local judge previously indicted for accepting bribes and payoffs was found dead at his home this morning of a single gunshot wound. The weapon used in the death has not been located, but it appears to have been a suicide.

The judge had made a statement to the press immediately following his indictment that he would not go down alone. He would name others involved in this activity.

He was awaiting sentencing following his indictment. Further investigation into his death will continue.

My judge? Was he the mysterious caller from long ago? The media reported that no weapon was found but it appeared to be a suicide. How did a man die of suicide then dispose of his own weapon? Another attempt to cover up the truth. Would the deception never end?

Since refusing to meet with the person claiming to be a judge two years ago the calls had stopped. The nightmare was left behind and I was determined that it should remain there. I refused to let this article upset me and even though several pages followed regarding the judge's life and judicial activities, I did not wish to read them. I continued to browse through the newspaper when a small but impressive notice caught my eye.

Engagement
Laird - Noland

Alpharetta - Judge Henry Laird and Linda Laird announce the engagement of their daughter, Noel to Larry Noland, son of Mr. and Mrs. Larry Noland, Sr.

Only two years? How could he do this? *Stop now! You will have nothing to do with this. It's over. Forget it. But her body hasn't been found.* My thoughts churned and the sense of justice fueled a fire in my soul.

Angrily tossing the newspaper on the table, I walked to the edge of the veranda and stared at the rocks below. Why did Sheri Noland plague me so? Tormented with these thoughts I walked back into my house, slammed the door, and sat down by the fireplace gazing into its shimmering light. As if on cue and to show me that I could not banish her from my life, the glowing firelight dimmed, and in its place once again was the unending vision of Sheri Noland. Her body, wrapped in a black tarp, was balanced precariously on the shoulders of two men, one with sandy hair, and the other, stringy, black hair and a beard. They carried her body through the woods behind the timber site, but unlike the previous vision they did not stop in the woods. As the trees began to thin, they walked out into a clearing, facing a stone walled rock quarry filled with cerulean, blue water. The two men laid her body on a large rock jutting out over the water, tied nylon rope around the tarp-wrapped bundle and secured a large rock to the rope. They lowered the body over the side of the quarry wall and let go of the rope. Weighted by the rock the body fell heavily into the water as the two figures diabolically grinned at each other.

"They won't never find that broad," one said to the other.

"They'll still be looking for her years from now," the other said laughing.

Neither man bothered to take a second look as they turned and retraced their steps through the woods.

"Look closer," the familiar voice commanded.

I peered over the edge of the rock wall into the quarry and I was shown what they had not cared to see. The end of the rope had become lodged in the crevice of a large rock on its way down into the quarry. Sheri's body was buried in the watery grave, but held securely by the rope caught in the crevice.

"Now what will you do?" Sheri asked.

CHAPTER NINETEEN

New Year's Eve arrived with renewed energy and excitement. A few months earlier Jon and I purchased a ninety-three year old Craftsman-styled house in a wonderful, gracious, historic neighborhood. New Year's Eve was the perfect time to share our quaint home with friends who would appreciate it as we did. Filled with the character and ambiance of an elegant time past, our home was comforting. The rooms, spacious and flowing with walls placed at odd angles lent a mysterious flair to the structure. The crackling of the cozy fire filled the air and warmed the soul. Aroma from homemade bread baking in the oven teased our nostrils, and made our mouths water in anticipation. Our friends' eyes were bright and their voices cheerful as they greeted us at the door. It was a wonderful evening and all else was forgotten.

An interesting mix of personalities — a research librarian, a homemaker, three lawyers and two executives, all of whom we enjoyed were invited to our home. We proudly showed them through our distinctive home while they asked interesting questions about the renovation process. There was much laughter as we talked about our many errors with painting and plumbing. The descriptions of our blunders prompted personal stories from our guests that lasted throughout the late supper.

Our guests retired to the parlor around the fire for coffee and dessert. One of our friends found me in the kitchen placing the last dollop of whipped cream on a pie.

"Lynn, you have a latecomer to the party. She's standing in the parlor by the stairs."

I did not know who would be arriving so late because everyone we had invited was already present. I walked into the parlor to say hello to the new arrival but stopped in my tracks. I could not believe my own eyes. Standing quietly by the stair landing was Sheri Noland, or at least someone who looked like Sheri Noland. She did not move or speak and she appeared hazy as though she was standing in a shadow. My friends were trying to talk to her in an attempt to make her feel welcome, but she did not respond.

"Lynn, who is this young woman? She looks very familiar," one of them whispered.

I struggled with how to tell them and questioned if I should even try. But they could see her and I could not just ignore the fact that she was standing in my parlor. I had to say something to my guests that would not alarm them.

"Can all of you see her?" I questioned.

They looked at me as though I had lost my mind. All nodded but none understood the reason for my question.

"The young woman you see is Sheri Noland. You remember she was abducted several years ago and no one was able to find her after the ransom was paid. She's presumed dead."

They stared at me, then at her and convinced that I was playing a joke on them began to laugh. Earlier in the evening we had discussed how everyone thought old houses were haunted, and all of them knowing my eccentric sense of humor, thought this was a planned part of the evening. It was not.

"Sheri, why are you here?" I asked calmly and with concern for my ethereal friend.

With a soft but determined voice that brought a chill to the room she answered. "Because you left me. Please help me, Lynn. You're my only hope."

What could I say to her? I had struggled the last couple of years to make her go away and she was right. I had left her. I needed my life back.

Our friends stared at her as they realized this was not a joke.

They were in the same room with a spirit and not only could they see her, they could hear her. They all sat in total disbelief at the phenomenon they were witnessing.

"Lynn, what's going on here? How is this possible? Jon, does this kind of thing happen in your house often?"

While everyone in the room asked questions, no one noticed that Sheri was gone. She had vanished just as she appeared.

Jon looked at me with amusement, his eyes twinkling. "Honey, I think you might try explaining this." He was thoroughly enjoying the astonished looks on our guests' faces, and waiting to hear my explanation. He had gotten used to strange things happening around me and nothing shocked him easily, but our friends had never experienced anything like this.

"She's gone!" exclaimed one of our guests and everyone looked around the room in awe.

"Lynn, explain! Start at the beginning. We know there's quite a story here and we're all waiting."

The remainder of our New Year's evening was spent engrossed in the epic saga of Sheri Noland and my clairvoyant visions. We even forgot to toast in the New Year as midnight came and went. Because these people were our friends, I was not uncomfortable sharing this experience with them. None of them could disbelieve. They had all seen and heard her.

* * * *

After unsuccessfully struggling numerous times to remove Sheri Noland from my life, once again I placed a call to Wayne Hilliard. Sheri's visit and her plea on New Year's Eve gave me no choice.

"Mr. Hilliard, this is Lynn Conley. Do you remember me? We haven't spoken in some time."

"Yes, Lynn, I remember you. How are you?" he said with the same gentleness as before.

"I'm well, thanks. I'd like to speak with you again if you don't mind. Can I meet with you in the next few days if that's convenient?"

"Sure, I think that's possible. Let me check my schedule to see when I have some time." We arranged the time and place just like before, only this time I was driving to his home in Madison, Tennessee.

On the long drive to Mr. and Mrs. Hilliard's home I mentally recalled what I had been shown in the visions over the last several years. Most of it made extraordinary sense, but I continued to be affected by deep emotional ties to Sheri Noland and that concerned me. With the passing of time I thought the emotions would have run their course, but they had not.

As I drove through the picturesque city with its historical buildings and antiquated churches, forgotten memories stirred. I passed an elementary school and remembered my daughter attending there for a short time. Only a few blocks further, I drove past the church my family had attended and where my son attended kindergarten. I smiled at the pleasant memories there for I had taught the children's choir. It was so long ago I had almost forgotten. We had lived in this wonderful town a short time. Jon's company transferred him so often many of the cities ran together over time.

I drove around the city for a while unable to find the street where the Hilliards lived. I drove past the post office, turned around and drove back into the parking lot. A postal clerk should know the location of a street and be able to help me with directions. The line inside was long and I waited impatiently for my turn.

"Can you tell me where to find this street address?" I asked the clerk and showed her my hand written directions.

"I'm sorry but I don't know," she answered offhand.

"Do you have a city map?"

"We do but it's in the back and I can't leave to go get it."

"Would you happen to know where Wayne and Sarah Hilliard live?" I thought because of the vast media coverage of the kidnapping she might recognize the name.

She shook her head.

A man several feet behind me stepped out of line and walked up to the counter.

"I know where they live," he said and pointed across the street. "Go two streets up and turn right. Their house is the first one on the right where the street dead-ends."

He walked away as I said, "Thank you," and instead of returning to his place in line walked out of the post office and disappeared in the parking lot. I smiled thinking nothing surprised me these days, got back into my car and followed his directions.

Continuing to observe the neighborhoods, I realized that the Hilliards' house was a few blocks from the house where we had lived years ago, and something was tugging at my memory. I drove into the Hilliards' driveway and with smiling faces they were waiting for me at the front door. They made me feel very welcome as we sat down in their living room. Again, I wondered why I was involved in their lives. I glanced around the beautifully decorated room and noticed photographs of Sheri and Beth placed on tables throughout. Mrs. Hilliard said how nice it was to see me again although I knew we had never met. She looked at me curiously as though she was trying to understand something.

"Lynn, did you join us in the organized search for Sheri?" she asked.

"No, I always searched on my own," I said wondering why she kept scrutinizing me.

As though to answer my unspoken question she said, "I know that we've met and I'm trying to think where it might have been.

"Mr. Hilliard and I met several years ago, but you were not with him. I'm sorry I don't know when it might have been."

I began telling them about the percolating memories as I passed by schools and churches on the way to their home; how my family and I had lived in this city for a very short time and in what area.

Knowing that they had been residents for many years, I asked if they knew Ms. Martin who had once been my wonderful neighbor.

"Oh my God, I do know you!" Mrs. Hilliard burst out. "You lived across the street from my parents. We met in my mother's kitchen over tea and cookies, and you were with the neighbor you just mentioned."

She stared at me with a look of disbelief. Mr. Hilliard looked first at her then at me, not understanding this conversation any more than I did. I did not remember her or her mother or the event she was describing at first.

"Lynn, that particular day …" She paused in mid-sentence as though painfully remembering and then continued. "Lynn, Sheri was with me that day at my mothers."

Sarah Hilliard looked away with such sadness in her eyes I thought my heart would break for her. She stared at the walls as if that made remembering less painful.

"She was only twelve years old. Sheri was fascinated with your green eyes and talked about you for weeks after that day, and she was surprisingly sad when you moved away. Her attachment to you always puzzled me because she didn't really know you that well."

My breath hung suspended in my throat as the images of Mrs. Hilliard's words began to penetrate my memory. I knew why Sheri Noland had seemed so familiar in the visions as I now remembered that day. I thought about the young girl with whom I had shared such a strange bond many years ago. Why had I not remembered her or at least recognized the name? Too many years and too many moves cause memories to fade. I finally understood my obsessive need to help Sheridan Hilliard Noland. My eyes glistened with tears and I turned my head away so the Hilliards could not see.

We touch lives unknowingly and our own lives are intertwined with those we meet along the way, never fully realizing the impact we may have on each other's destiny. Now I understand why she would not leave me alone. I understand completely.

I began to tell them what had transpired since my last meeting with Mr. Hilliard's investigators so many years ago. I told them about the visions and the rock quarry, the telephone calls from the alleged judge, the unwelcomed visitors invading my home, fear for my family's safety, and last but not least, Sheri's appearance at my home on New Year's Eve. They listened without comment. The passing years had conditioned them to react without outward emotion to any news of their daughter.

"The Canton police have informed us that they received a confession from a man in prison who says he helped Daniel Spicer with the kidnapping, and he buried Sheri's body," Mr. Hilliard said. "I don't know whether he did or not, but he gave directions to an area that's about fifty miles northeast of Canton. My investigator and I plan to search the area as soon as possible."

There was nothing I could say. It was not good news for someone to tell you that they buried your daughter's body, but at the same time, it would put closure to the search.

"Bob Wyliff is my investigator, and I would like for him to call you in a few days to arrange a search for the quarry you saw in your visions, just in case we don't find anything." Mr. Hilliard said. "I won't discount any leads until I've investigated them."

I was not sure what I expected from the Hilliards, or for that matter, even what I was doing there. I still had nothing conclusive to give them. Both gave me a hug and thanked me for the information. I left their house feeling sad and ineffective once again, and I desperately wished I could help them solve this horrible crime.

Driving home quiet and pensive I thought about my own feelings. How would I hold onto reality if it were my daughter or son? I know I would not be as strong as they. The loss of a child regardless of their age leaves a gaping hole in the parents' world that can never be filled. As I considered their pain, tears began to trickle down my cheeks.

"Sheri, if this man's confession is real, do I need to do anything else?" I asked out loud now knowing she would hear me.

In the silence of the dark surrounding me I heard the familiar voice again, and I felt her presence in my car.

"Don't let my daddy quit. Go north."

* * * *

Through considerable effort over the next few days, I located an aerial map and began to search for rock quarries. The map showed approximately fifteen in the general area of County Road 249. They were designated on the map legend as quarries or pits. I marked each one numerically on the map based on distance, and waited for the investigator's telephone call that Mr. Hilliard had promised. Two days later the call came and the investigator wanted to come to my house for a discussion. I agreed, but reluctantly gave him my address. The previous investigators had not lasted long so I was curious about this one. Mr. Hilliard felt confident that Bob Wyliff was sincere in his efforts, but something deep within my soul cautioned me to be careful. I knew I was overreacting now suspicious of anyone involved in this case.

The doorbell rang and I opened the wooden door but kept the glass door closed between us. I saw a small man, completely unobtrusive and grandfatherly standing on my front porch.

He smiled and said, "Hi, Lynn. I'm Bob Wyliff."

"Do you have identification?"

He grinned somewhat surprised, but then showed me his driver's license and private investigator license. After examining them I opened the glass door to allow him in.

"Sorry, nothing personal," I said. "I just don't take chances."

We sat on the sofa and made small talk for a while getting to know each other. I needed to feel confident that I could trust this man before I showed him the map. We discussed Mr. and Mrs. Hilliard, Sheri Noland and his involvement in the case. He seemed to be genuine and expressed his concern about the FBI and local police department's inability to solve the case. He spoke of his investigative team and how closely they worked together. I finally showed Mr. Wyliff the map outlining each of the areas, and he decided that we needed to take a look at all of them. We scheduled the search for two weeks later, giving him time to investigate the other area with Mr. Hilliard. After three years there did not seem to be any urgency.

Bob Wyliff was detained with previous responsibilities and sent his associates to accompany me on the search for the quarries. I had borrowed a friend's Jeep to prevent anyone from following me, still paranoid from past experience. Not wanting to reveal my identity to anyone other than the investigators, as a safety precaution I pulled my hair back into a ponytail and hid it under a baseball cap so that I looked like a boy, and I drove to Canton to meet the investigators. I had given Bob Wyliff a description of the Jeep, and he and his associates were waiting for me in the designated parking lot.

"Hi, Lynn," Mr. Wyliff said. "This is Bill, my grandson. He's working on the case with me and he's very qualified. This is Al. He's an investigator with over twenty years experience. They'll both take good care of you."

As I shook hands with each of them, Mr. Wyliff continued, "I'm meeting with the sheriff in a few minutes so I can't go with you."

I wondered why Bob Wyliff was meeting with the sheriff and if his meeting was about Sheri. Something about him did not sit right with me, although I had no idea what it was other than a feeling. Al and Bill got into the Jeep and studied the map, then suggested we start with the closest quarry. We drove into a secluded mountainous area well known to the police for its car theft rings and auto chop shops. We had considerable difficulty locating the correct roads because the signs had been removed, and finally we happened upon a blocked dirt road that was consistent with the map. We left the Jeep and began on foot walking the three-mile road toward the first quarry. Nothing about this area looked or felt right. The road climbed spiraling around a small mountain and then down into a valley. Brush beside the road had recently burned and the ashes were still smoldering adding heat to the already sweltering day. Someone carelessly burning trash or disposing of a cigarette had set the fire. It was unnaturally quiet as we walked, only the sounds of our labored breathing and our footsteps could be heard.

"Perhaps just a little further around the next bend we'll find something," Bill said, wiping sweat from his forehead with the back of his hand.

"I hope so," I responded gasping for air. "This hike is killing me."

Around the next turn in the road we found water, but this was not what I had seen in the visions. The area was filled with trash and had been used for many years as a dumping ground. It certainly was the kind of place one could hide a body, but it was not the right place. We turned around and started the long hike back.

On the way back to the Jeep Al found a strange looking object lying on the ground.

"Look at this," he said as he leaned down and picked it up. "It looks like a wooden carving, maybe it was a child's toy at one time."

Not knowing why, I looked at it closely. The head was clearly that of a lamb, but the body was broken with half of it missing. I unconsciously placed it in my pocket for safekeeping as we continued the long walk. No one had thought to bring a thermos of water and our mouths were parched. It had become more difficult to walk in the heat and we were forced to stop and rest. Our clothing was wet with sweat and clung to our bodies making us even more uncomfortable. I described the details of the quarry in the visions over and over again to the investigators as we rested hoping they would know of such a place.

"I'm not anxious to go back up that hill are you?" I asked Al and Bill.

They laughed and shook their heads, but there was no other way back. We finally reached the Jeep and left the area with one quick stop at McDonalds to quench our thirsts. We continued on searching for the next area marked on the map. It also was a pit, not a quarry, and our frustration was growing along with the heat.

Hours later Bill remembered a place consistent with what I had described, but it was not in the area of County Road 249, and it was not on my map. It was at least a half-hour drive north. Out of sheer frustration I agreed to take a look at it. We drove until County Road 249 came to a dead end then turned onto another county road and continued north. I watched closely as we drove into a more densely wooded area, and I noticed a timber site on the right just off the paved road.

"Bill, how old do you think that timber site is?" I asked remembering the one in the vision.

"Probably hasn't been worked in many years," he said. "See how grown up it is? And see all the old logs lying around? When they've cut all the timber they want they leave it like that."

Less than one-half mile further, we turned right onto a dirt road. As we drove further into the wooded area the road became impassable, filled with potholes, boulders and water.

"Careful, Lynn. You'll have to turn to the right slowly here or we might flip over," Bill said as the Jeep tilted on two wheels.

I heard a sigh of thankfulness coming from the backseat as the Jeep righted itself and sat firmly back down on the road. I maneuvered until we could go no further. The electrified air made me feel at odds with this environment as though I was about to go somewhere I knew I had already been, do something I had already done. We got out of the Jeep and walked a short distance through the woods until the trees began to thin. Before us appeared a large clearing, but we could not see beyond the blue of the sky as though the earth ceased at that moment. A few more steps and I clinched my eyes shut, held my breath, afraid to look, afraid not to look. I felt it — I knew — I had walked right into the vision.

I opened my eyes without needing this physical sight. The rocks were in exact proportion to the water and to the wooded area as in the last vision. Before me rose the boulder overlooking the quarry on which I had seen Sheri Noland standing each time she asked, "Will you help me?" I stood in reverent silence and awe for what seemed an eternity absorbing every detail.

"Al, do you know of any old shacks in these woods?" I whispered.

"There's a couple of hunting shacks around here," he said with a querulous look.

"There's one less than a mile through the woods from here," Bill said. "I think it's been abandoned for years though. Hunters don't come up here as much as they used to."

I went to the familiar rock overlooking the quarry and gazed down into the icy blue water. As far as I could see the walls were a solid sheet of rock, and it was at least forty foot to the water's surface. The exquisite beauty of this place contradicted the ghastliness of Sheri Noland's brutal murder. So overwhelmed by emotions that I could do nothing else, I sat down on the massive rock and wept. I asked the investigators to give me some time alone. They understood and walked away to begin searching the woods. For a long time I stayed on the rock inhaling the awesome beauty of the surroundings, remembering the visions.

"Sheri, if you're here you must show me something," I whispered needing confirmation.

"Look into the water," the familiar voice said.

Directly below were two boulders beneath the surface of the water. To the right of the boulders something that appeared to be a rope was caught in the crevice of one of them.

"Bill, will you come over here and take a look at this?" I yelled out to the younger investigator who was staring out at the water. "What is that?" I asked as he walked over.

"Looks to me like some sort of rope or cable."

"How deep do you think the water is right there?"

"Probably thirty feet or more to where that rope is caught. The water always distorts your perception."

He leaned over the rock further to get a better look. "Really looks like a rope that's pulled taut. Like something is holding it from below," he said with a quizzical look. He turned to walk away from the rock for a better view and stopped.

"Lynn, look at this."

Carved into the same rock on which we stood overlooking the quarry, was the head of a lamb identical to the broken wooden carving found earlier today at the pit.

"The sacrificial lamb," I said in disbelief. "What do you think this means?"

"Looks like a sign to me," he said, shrugged his shoulders and grinned.

I shook my head and laughed realizing that he was teasing me. I walked away from the rock and into the woods for a view from a different angle. Everything looked right, everything felt right, but something was missing. The quarry was one more piece of the puzzle, yet pieces were still missing. I felt uneasy, but I did not understand why. Maybe it was the eeriness of this place, as though the air around us had no breath. I took pictures of the area using a special infrared film that captures the emission of energy forms. Looking through the lens I angled the camera to get the best possible picture of the rock, but something was obstructing my view. I repositioned the camera and looked again at the rock jutting out over the quarry. An energy or an illumination much like you would see with heat rising from a stove, or the glow around a candle's flame, was rising from the rock. I shook my head trying to clear my vision and looked again only to discover it was still there. I looked through the lens at other rocks but the image was not present. A white-gold shimmering essence of a figure that I did not see on any of the other rocks stood motionless. I began taking pictures focusing on the illumination as I moved around trying to avoid the sun's glare. I did not want anything to interfere with the clarity of these pictures. The investigators watched me from a distance but did not interrupt. Hours passed without notice. The silence was deafening.

I needed to see the hunting shack, but I could not insist that we go there today. Instinct was holding me back confusing my thoughts, and I continued to feel that something was not quite right.

"What do you want us to do? Is this the right area? Should we get divers in here to check it out?" asked one of the investigators.

"Let's do nothing right now," I said. "I need to sort something out. I think we need to have the divers search the quarry, but not yet."

Surprised by my response, I wondered if I had revealed too much of my own confusion. I could not seem to rid myself of the feeling that the investigators may not be what they seemed. Had I become too suspicious of everyone? These men were here to help. They had no hidden agenda. This was their profession and I reprimanded myself for questioning their motives. After all, my own motives were somewhat removed from reality these days. Who was I to question anyone?

Too tired to maneuver the Jeep back through the maze of ruts, I asked Bill if he would drive and I climbed into the back seat. As we drove out of the area back onto the paved road we passed a large billboard. "VOTE FOR LAMB." Bill began to laugh and tease me.

"There's another lamb. That now makes three we've seen today."

Once again the word "sacrifice" scrolled across my mind. We continued our way back to civilization passing a pasture filled with sheep and lamb. I closed my eyes wanting to shut out the world, the fear, and the life altering visions. I wanted peace and I wanted Sheri's body to be found and I wanted to be like normal people. I fell asleep for the remainder of the trip and awoke an hour later hearing Bill's voice.

"Sorry, but you have to drive yourself home. This is as far as we go. It's been interesting to say the least. Let me know when you're ready for the divers. Get some rest, Lynn, you look exhausted."

Entering my house at the end of our long day, I picked up a book entitled You Have A Purpose - Begin It Now from its resting place on the coffee table. Almost ceremoniously I closed my eyes, opened the book to a random page, opened my eyes and read a quote from Winston Churchill: "Men stumble over the truth from time to time, but most pick themselves up and hurry off as if nothing happened."

Was that what I had done today? Had I stumbled over the truth and hurried off as if nothing happened? *Go back to the county road you saw in the first visions and you'll find the missing piece.* How do I know this? From what source does this information come?

I walked into the dining room and spread the map out on the table for another look. If I drew a line extending up from the ending of County Road 249 to the area of the quarry that we searched today it would be directly NORTH. *Lynn, pay attention. North!*

I searched frantically again on the map in the area of County Road 249. Another pit or quarry was marked. How had I missed that one? Neither the investigators nor I had seen it on the map at all today. Was this the missing piece?

Two days later I drove back to the area of County Road 249 that I had not traveled in more than three years. There were no concrete tiles on either side of the road now. Construction had been completed since the first visions. Following the map I drove to a side road clearly marked by a road sign and made the turn. Three or four miles further I saw a large fence with posted warning signs forbidding entry to a coal mine, but there were no guards. The gate was open and I drove through as if I belonged there.

As far as I could see there were enormous rock mountains. The site was desolate, ashen in color, and appeared to be abandoned. I drove over a graveled road up to the top of a mountain then stopped the car. Before me was the most incredible rock wall I had ever seen, a smaller version of the Grand Canyon, its beauty breathtaking. I walked around trying to get a feel for the area, but there was nothing unusual. I stared at the rock wall trying to imprint it in my mind because I could not believe that such a place existed hidden away like a fantasy.

Back down the mountain I saw another road leading through a pass. Rock mountains flanked either side of the pass, and another rock wall appeared as beautiful as the previous one. I shivered even though the air was warm, and I remembered an old wives' tale that someone was walking over your grave when you shivered for no reason. Not a pleasant thought at this moment, in this place alone.

The vast rock wall extended downward and I walked to the edge to look over. Water cascaded halfway down the wall into an old rock quarry. The quarry's sides had caved in over the years and its pool was shallow. I stood in wonder at the beautiful surroundings and yet at the same time I was troubled. The uneasy feeling that I experienced working with the investigators two days earlier surfaced again. The rocks began to appear encased in a fog and as though I had stepped through time, I went back five years.

Daniel Spicer had brought Sheri here after her final telephone call to Larry. I saw the bearded man with dark, stringy hair shove Sheri into a pick-up and take her to a shack deep within the woods. I saw all of the events as they happened in sequence, and then I understood why this area was important. Sheri was guiding me through her final hours, and they began here. Daniel Spicer had turned Sheri over to the hired killer instructing him to take her to the woods and let her go. I knew now that I had to go to the hunting shack in the woods to see and feel what had taken place there. I must walk in Sheri's footsteps from the timber site through the woods to the quarry for there was something along the way that she wanted me to see.

Once more I heard the cascading water and my vision cleared. Making my way back to the car I drove out of the area and headed for home. On the way I stopped by the photo store to pick up the pictures I had taken at the rock quarry two days earlier. I questioned the experts at the photo lab about the film. Were they sure there was no light leak in the camera? Were they sure the film had no defects? They guaranteed me that the film and the processing were correct and there were no problems, and then they wanted to know who the ghosts were in the photos and where they were taken. I laughed and said I could never tell them.

I placed the photos in my bag not daring to look at them until I had reached the safety of my home. I was anxious to see if the infrared film really could capture images not visible to the naked eye especially since the photo lab employees were so inquisitive. Once secure in my house with the door locked I opened the envelopes.

The images were perfect with a surreal appearance. The film had captured the essence of whatever I saw standing on the rock overlooking the quarry. One photo was especially disturbing. In the water beneath the rock overlooking the quarry was the image of a body. It was in the same area where I had seen a rope caught in the crevice of the rocks in the vision. The face appeared to be partially decomposed and no longer contained in the wrapping, but the outline of the body was irrefutable. I scrutinized the photo from every possible angle, but the image remained the same. I ran to the kitchen, grabbed the phone and called Mr. Hilliard. Unable to reach him, I called Bob Wyliff the investigator.

* * * *

The doorbell rang at exactly twelve thirty the following day as I was finishing my lunch. Bob Wyliff walked in with a smile on his face when I opened the front door. He thought we had become comrades in our fight against evil. Relying on his conventional, logical evidence, he had joined forces with me, using my non-conventional clairvoyant visions as his guidance.

"Hi, how are you? You wanted to show me the pictures?"

"Yes, I'm anxious to know what you see," I said.

He walked into the dining room not waiting for me, pulled out a chair to make himself comfortable, and began to look at the photos spread out on the table. He studied them not wanting to miss any details. He held each one up to the sunlight beaming through the windows, turned them from side to side, angle to angle, and like me, he could not believe what he saw. I watched him as he studied the photos, still trying to decide if I could trust him. That uneasy feeling was constant when I was in his company, even though he had done nothing to cause these feelings, and I simply would not force myself to tell him everything I knew.

"Lynn, this looks like a body in this picture!" he proclaimed with shock. He looked up at me with surprise on his face and whispered, "Do you know what you've got here? You make sure the negatives are hidden away so no one can get to them. I'd like to take a couple of these with me. Do you mind? I'd like to show them to an expert and get his opinion."

"Sure, but you don't let anything happen to them, and do not let them get into the wrong hands."

"You know I wouldn't do that. I'll call you after I've shown them to a couple of people," he said defensively then placed them in his folder and started for the door.

"We need to make arrangement for the trip to the hunting shack soon," I said.

"There is an urgency to see it now, and Bill and Al seem to be the only ones who know where it is," I said as I walked him to his car.

Bob Wyliff called me later in the day to tell me that his experts all agreed. The image in the picture was indeed a body. Based on that information he had decided to make preparations to schedule a dive into the water of the quarry. He would call me once the arrangements were completed. Mr. Hilliard had instructed him to handle everything and he could not wait for me to decide when or if the dive should take place. He wanted it done immediately and he reminded me that he was the investigator, and it was his case. He also had arranged the trip to the hunting shack as I had requested, and we would travel there tomorrow morning. It was pointless for me to voice any objection.

I placed a call to the university hospital and spoke with a forensic pathologist. I needed to know how great the decomposition of a body would be five years after death if it were submersed in thirty-degree water.

CHAPTER TWENTY

I have often wished for a switch on the human body that would turn off uninvited thoughts. A clear mind was needed today not one muddled with insecurities. I felt strongly that we would find the shack hidden within the woods, but again driving to meet the investigators I was filled with apprehension. Bob Wyliff and his associates, Bill and Al, were waiting patiently for me when I drove into the parking lot of the old country store where we had arranged to meet. We rode together to a dirt road only a short distance from the quarry, and I was reminded as we traveled of the terrain and the sounds Sheri might have heard along the way.

The shack was secluded in the woods away from the road, and one would have to know of its existence to find it. Its structure was dark and foreboding with a disintegrating tin roof and partially covered windows. The musty scent of moss and decaying leaves filled my nostrils as we inched our way through the light-filtered woods, respectful of any snakes that might have taken up residence in the dense undergrowth. The wind began to gust with a howling sound that reminded me of wolf packs, twisting the tree limbs and I shivered with a mysterious fear.

Even before we reached it, my movements froze as I sensed the horrible energy surrounding the shack that was staring at us through the trees. Seeing this ghastly place in the visions did not sufficiently prepare me to physically see it.

Against my will I crept into the sagging doorway of the shack's decomposing porch and peered into the dimly lit interior. It smelled of rot and filth and the odor caused my stomach to churn. An ugly, black spider the size of my hand was hugging the door, staring angrily at me as though I were trespassing. Giving my eyes time to adjust to the lack of light, I entered the main area of the shack from the porch. Incredible sadness overwhelmed me as I continued to inch my way just inside the door, but that was as far as I could go. I could not enter this room.

Sunlight filtered through the holes in the tin roof and played kaleidoscopic games on the dingy floor. Worn, discarded mattresses covered much of it and made a comfortable nest for the rats. I saw Sheri in the dimness of the corner of the room, her arms tied behind her, her mouth gagged as she had appeared in the visions. She was slumped over sideways with a look of hopelessness in her eyes. I knew that I saw her through the memory of the vision because she was not physically present. My eyes filled with acidic tears and I fought to choke back sobs. My heart was breaking for this young woman who had prayed until the last moment that someone would find her. I could feel the horror that had taken place here and I could hear her painful sobbing. Unable to bear this sight no longer, I turned back, and had my limbs cooperated, I would have run out into the light. Instead with forced movement I made my way back into the woods. Behind the shack stood a covered lean-to, its floor made of rotting leaves and another worn mattress. From an altered sight I witnessed the depraved men raping and brutalizing Sheri there under the lean-to, her eyes filled with terror as the waves of blackness engulfed her. I fell to my knees, lifted my face toward the heavens and cried, "Dear God, why? How could this happen?"

These despicable men responsible for her brutal treatment must be punished — all of them. I felt emotionally shattered and at that moment I made a silent vow. Our law had failed miserably in its attempt to teach decency to others and it needed help. Justice would prevail even if it took a lifetime to accomplish. I felt that I owed Sheri because I was unable to help her even with my gift in time. With great effort I made my way back to the porch of the shack and to the investigators.

Bob Wyliff was searching through the rubble lying on the floor while Bill and Al walked around in the woods. Rain-splattered, blank notebook paper was scattered about. I was sure it was the source of the paper on which Karen, the bearded man's girlfriend, had written the names of those responsible for Sheri's death. My foot hit something in the dinginess of the floor, and I used the toe of my boot to slide it out into the light. Examining it with my eyes only not daring to touch it with my hands, I saw hair and fibers stuck to the partially dirt-covered duct tape that I had uncovered. Sheri had now shown us what we needed to see along the path of her final hours. Bob Wyliff bagged the duct tape for testing, along with other items we found that might be used as evidence. Just in case my gut feeling was correct about Mr. Wyliff, I concealed a piece of the tape in my pocket for testing by a person of my choosing.

I took one last painful look at this tomb where Sheri Noland was held captive imprinting it in my mind, and with trembling legs walked out into the sunlight where there was hope.

* * * *

Today the divers would search the quarry and I must prepare myself to face it. I was not sure how I felt at this moment. Scared? Relieved? My actions had been guided by the visions, and obviously by Sheri for a very long time. I knew that some day there would be a conclusion and I wanted it to be Sheri's body in the water, but at the same time I was anxious. I had seen her as a whole person throughout her kidnapping and subsequent death, and I had come to know her through the visions as a real person, my friend. Her physical appearance would be altered and I did not wish to see my friend that way, but I also knew that I must be present for this final resurrection. Sheri would not have it any other way. I thought about my discussion two weeks before with a forensic pathologist when I had questioned him about the decomposition of Sheri's body. He had said if the water was cold enough the body could be preserved with minimal damage for several years. I questioned how the water would damage the note in her pocket and his response was encouraging. Even if the water had seeped into the tarp wrapping and destroyed the ink on the paper, the chemical remains of the ink could be analyzed through an intricate process, and the note would be legible enough to read. I was ecstatic with this information because even years later an expert would uncover the names of those responsible for Sheri's murder. She would still have her day in court — and justice would prevail.

Mr. Hilliard had collected many pieces of the puzzle including the names of those present at the party the night his daughter overheard the conversation that had sealed her fate. He was so close to the truth. Finding her body with its concealed, incriminating evidence would destroy those responsible, but would it ever bring peace to the hearts of those who had loved and lost her? I did not think so.

Wayne and Sarah Hilliard would not be present this day. They could not bear the possibility of another disappointment. There had been so many. They also could not watch their daughter's body being withdrawn from its watery tomb, should it be recovered. Bob Wyliff was given full authority to do whatever he deemed necessary with the dive and I hoped the Hilliards had not placed their faith in the wrong people in their desperate need to know the truth. Sheridan Hilliard Noland, the sacrificial lamb, had guided us to this very day, and I had no doubts she would make sure the guilty were known and punished accordingly. Her strength and determination had grown for five years, and I knew she would have little compassion for anyone who tried to stop her efforts. The morning sky shrouded with grey and threatening clouds, added a sense of gloom to the listless air. Alone I drove up the winding road to meet the investigators for what I hoped would be our last time, and I was filled with sadness. I wanted to turn my car around and go home, back to safety, but I knew I could not. I was frightened, not for myself, but for Sheri's family, frightened of their emotions when they had to identify their daughter's remains.

The investigators were waiting with eager smiles as I drove into the parking lot and I thought that was odd. This was not a day of celebration for most of us. Other men were there that I failed to recognize, walking around outside the store as if they were also waiting for someone or something to arrive. Diving gear was laying in the back of an all terrain vehicle parked in the lot. Another all terrain vehicle drove into the lot and a large man, dressed in jeans and a tee shirt stepped out to join the others as though he knew them well. I watched in wonder as yet another and still another vehicle drove into the lot.

I was concerned with the activity taking place outside the store because there were too many people. This search was supposed to be quiet and private. Who had invited all of these people? The county sheriff in full uniform, stepped out of his car and announced to everyone present that he had arrived with his deputies. There was now a full audience, and I found myself searching for the television camera crew that I was sure had also been invited.

"Lynn, good morning," Bob Wyliff said. "We're just about ready to go. I think everyone has made it. We're waiting on the paramedic who should be here in a few minutes." He had no audible concern in his voice.

"Who are all these people?" I questioned not wanting anyone else to hear. "These three men are part of the diving team and the other divers will meet us at the quarry. This is Sheriff Hill from Cherokee County and one of his deputies. The one in uniform is Sheriff Redfield from Gilmer County with his deputies."

"Bob, I don't understand. Why are they here? This search was supposed to be confidential."

"It's a matter of legal jurisdiction. Sheri was kidnapped in Cherokee County so their sheriff needed to be here. This quarry is in

Gilmer County so their sheriff had to be present. We don't need legal problems when the body is found."

"And the diving team?"

"They're part of Gilmer County's Drug Task Force Unit, all certified. Again, it's their county."

My heart sank. What was this man doing? We were not required legally to have anyone present unless and until a body was recovered, and only at that time were we required to call the sheriffs and the medical examiner to witness the event, and Gilmer County's Drug Task Force Unit? Hadn't Wyliff heard any of the rumors that some of them were involved in drug trafficking and maybe even their sheriff? Why not a private diving team, one that had no involvement whatsoever? No law required us to use the county's divers. I could not understand the workings of Bob Wyliff's mind, and that familiar uneasiness ever present when I was in the company of the investigators, was pounding away at my intuition. Screaming in fact.

"Lynn, I'd like you to meet Sheriff Redfield and Sheriff Hill. This is Lynn, one of my investigators. She's been working with me on this case for several years." Bob made polite introductions and walked away to speak with someone else. Thank God he did not call me a psychic.

"You're not going to find a body in that water. We've looked here before. There's nothing I assure you," Sheriff Redfield arrogantly stated, grinned and then strutted away not waiting for a response.

"Lynn, I saw the picture you took and I agree that it's a body in the water. I think she's down there," Sheriff Hill stated looking around as if he did not want to be heard.

The paramedic arrived and the full caravan began its descent into the woods. I sat paralyzed in the passenger seat of Bill's vehicle wanting to turn back, knowing we would not accomplish our goal. These divers could never allow her body to be recovered with its incriminating evidence if they were involved. My thoughts were running rampant. What could I do? How could I prevent what my gut feeling told me was about to happen? I felt responsible and angry with myself for not paying closer attention to my apprehension about the investigators. We drove the final distance, entered the dirt road to the quarry, parked and got out of the vehicles. Other people were already present waiting for us, none of whom I knew. A motorboat sped past on the water as its passengers craned their necks to see who was present on the rocks. Sheriff Redfield strutted around telling jokes and tales of his personal diving experiences in these very waters as the divers prepared to enter the blue tomb. I mindfully watched each person while trying to understand his or her reason for being here. A couple of the men stayed just at the edge of the woods trying to stay out of the activity. I questioned Mr. Wyliff about the men, but he did not know who they were, and he was reluctant to ask them to leave.

The first diver entered the water, then the second, third and finally all were in. They began to swim over the surface surveying the area, adjusting their valves, and then disappeared beneath the water. Standing beside Sheriff Hill, I watched them, mesmerized by the bubbles. We stood on the rock, Sheri's rock, and with escalating anticipation waited.

"While we're alone, Lynn, I want to clarify something for you. I know you don't trust law enforcement from my county and rightly so, but you need to know why I'm here." Sheriff Hill's voice was soft as he gazed out at the water.

I listened half-heartedly wondering if this was yet another ploy. He continued speaking never shifting his eyes or turning his face away from the water.

"When Sheri was abducted I was working as an officer on Canton's police force, and I knew that many of the officers were on the take. I watched their mishandling of the investigation never saying anything to anyone about it, but I swore to myself that one day I would be in a position to do something. I loathed their behavior, but I knew I could do nothing then." He paused for a moment. "Well, now I'm in that position. After the FBI took over the case I left the police force and joined the Cherokee County Sheriff's Department as a deputy. That department also had corrupt deputies, but I kept my mouth shut and worked very hard to get to this point. Now I'm the Sheriff. I have one deputy that I trust with my life, and he and I are working outside the department on this case. This has become personal for me." He turned to look at me. "I trust you and your abilities but I need for you to trust me as well."

Staring out at the water not focused on anything in particular, I tried to digest his words. Sheriff Hill had an honest but stern face that framed his soft eyes. Why was his name never mentioned in all these years? I thought about all the officers and agents involved with the investigation and I could not place him. Did I dare believe him? Had I found someone with law enforcement who was trustworthy? I wanted to ask so many questions but this was not the time, and certainly not the place with so many people here. I would have to wait for a more appropriate time.

Bob Wyliff stood back away from the water's edge watching. He had a peculiar look on his face, one that was almost impossible to describe — a look of sadness and fear mixed with contentment. It deeply disturbed me. I was convinced that although he was not consciously aware of it, he was sabotaging his own investigation. I did not think that he had fallen prey to the corruption, but if Sheri's body was recovered, the investigation would be concluded and Wyliff's notoriety and income would come to an end. Had his professional judgment become tainted? Wyliff was almost seventy years old and making a name for himself was not important to him, but his ability to continue working and earning an income was.

Sheriff Redfield and one of his deputies continued to entertain the crowd with their exaggerated stories. The sheriff stood with one foot propped on a rock, the other solid on the ground, a profile of his boredom. The paramedic sat on a rock overlooking the water watching the diving team not wanting to be needed.

The divers emerged from the depths and took off their masks. They announced to the crowd that they were experiencing difficulty with their equipment, and they joked around and played on the water's surface like children in a bath. Almost an hour had passed and they had not yet begun to seriously search for the body.

"You should be diving over here," Sheriff Hill said, his arm extended and forefinger pointed to direct the head diver. "Why is your team searching way over there?"

"There's nothing where you point, Sheriff," stated the head diver.

"How do you know that if you don't look?" Sheriff Hill was annoyed with their playing around and so was I. Bob Wyliff watched from his perch on the upper side of the rocks as though he was unaware of any misconduct on the part of the divers. Irritated with Sherriff Hill but not wanting to appear insubordinate, the head diver put his mask back on and motioned for his team to go to the area the sheriff had indicated. They dove deeper and deeper into the water as we looked over the rock's edge trying to see them. We waited for them to return to the water's surface with Sheri's body, and we waited for the difficult emotions that would surely follow. Endless time, motionless air, and silence followed except for Sheriff Redfield's endless chatter. We waited in the agony of the moment for there was nothing else we could do.

The head diver soared up out of the water like a fountain and threw something at my feet. I was too startled to look down. Instead, I looked around to see who was watching only to discover that no one was except Sheriff Hill. Everyone else was engrossed in conversation and climbing around the upper part of the rocks bored with the activity below them. Inhaling a deep breath I summoned my courage and looked down to see what the diver had thrown at my feet. I gasped. A nylon cord cut in three separate places that had a dark stained loop large enough to go around a rock or a block or a body, lay at my feet. I dared not pick it up or move it. I stared at it.

"Here's your rope!" the head diver said. "I cut it loose there under the water." He motioned with his hand to the area where I had previously seen a rope caught in the crevice of a rock. "It was tied to a rock and wrapped around an old tree."

"That's great, but where's the body that it was attached to?" I asked without displaying any outward emotion. Inside I was raging, and why would he say, "here's *your* rope?"

"You'll never know." The head diver replied with a smirk, pulled his mask back over his face, and quickly disappeared under the water. I exhaled a deep, painful breath and looked at Sheriff Hill standing beside me on the rock. "Can't you do something?" I asked the sheriff as he stared at the rope.

"There's nothing I can do. This is not my jurisdiction and these are not my people. I'm not in charge any more than you are."

"Then why are you here?" I questioned rather hateful.

I clenched my teeth until my jaws ached. I was so angry my whole body shook. This was an anger so foreign to me that I could not begin to describe it. It was not only my anger I felt but Sheri's. She was seething. She knew what they had done then and now. The essence of her on the rock was growing stronger and stronger beside the sheriff and me, and we both felt her fury.

I picked up the rope and placed it inside my bag allowing no one to see me do this except Sheriff Hill. He said nothing and continued to watch Sheriff Redfield, Bob Wyliff and the others wander around the upper side of the rocks.

The divers emerged from the water. "We've wasted enough time here," the head diver shouted. "There's nothing down there except a bunch of old tires and trees. We're finished with this dive."

Their arrogance was intolerable. They climbed over the rocks out of the water and discarded their gear. Their expedition was over and they laughed and joked as they walked to their vehicles. The divers had made a grand show for all concerned and no one could say they had not done their job. Only I knew. Sheriff Hill knew. And the head diver knew. There remained a body hidden deep within the darkened rock ledges of the quarry now free from its confining rope.

"I guess they looked as best they could. Guess she wasn't down there after all. Well, we gave it our best shot," Bob Wyliff remarked as he turned and got into the marked car with Sheriff Redfield and drove away confirming my suspicion.

I stood on the rock still shaking with rage. How could we have gone this far; years of searching, years of pain and let these power hungry, drug pushing officials get away with this? I stared at the glowing essence of Sheri standing on the rock and words failed me. Nothing that I could say would make sense of this, yet I felt the need to say something. I was not sure if my words were for Sheri's comfort or mine.

"I'm so sorry, Sheri. I had no idea they would do this. The corruption just never ends. No one is immune to it."

I desperately wanted her to know that I had not abandoned her, but what had I accomplished? How had my visions helped anyone? At that moment I felt nothing but her rage surrounding me, and I did not know what to do. We could find another diving team, one that was incorruptible, and try again. Sheri's body was now under a ledge and immobile for the time being. They could not afford for it to drift away and be discovered. I took comfort in knowing that even as I questioned how I knew. How much pleasure had the head diver taken in throwing the rope at my feet? What kind of ego drives one to take chances such as this by flaunting hidden evidence? They were all so sure of themselves, but they would make mistakes as their arrogance took over. She would win.

I took one last look at the vast cavity, saw her spirit on the rock and heard her speak, words I will not forget the remainder of my life on this earth.

CHAPTER TWENTY-ONE

"I stand determined and unafraid here on this rock overlooking my somber, watery grave. I was a victim of their greed, their power and the corruption that accompanied the prosperity they gained through illegal actions, but I will not be a martyr for their cause." Sheri's voice grew stronger and I trembled.

"The people responsible for my death, how do they feel about themselves now five years later? Has anything changed in their lives? Oh, no doubt they have amassed considerable fortunes by now, but how do they feel inside? Do they have any remorse for their actions as they hide behind their political and legal masks? How many families have they destroyed? How many children have become addicted to illegal drugs as a result of their greed? Have they lost anyone they loved? Possibly a daughter? I wonder what goes through their minds as they lie down to sleep at night feeling confident that they have nothing to fear."

Sheri poured out her rage to the universe and I knew the angels wept for her for the sun hid its face behind the clouds, and the sky darkened its blue.

"I'm presumed to be dead but I know only the body dies. When the spirit is strong and determined it can transcend even the boundaries of death. It has been years since I was kidnapped and murdered and justice is not swift. She is blind because she must depend upon others and oftentimes they fail her. Except for the love and perseverance of my family and a dedicated few, she closed her eyes to the truth. Well, no more. Her eyes will be opened."

I stood trembling, staring at the rock and Sheri's ethereal image. She continued speaking but her essence had begun to weaken.

"As I give you these words, listen well. Those responsible for my demise have much to fear. You will be held accountable for your actions."

I strained my eyes to see her but her image was diminishing, and then she was gone.

I wept for the loss of my friend and for myself knowing I had failed her.

Everyone had gone and I sat there alone wondering why I had these visions. They had not helped Sheri so what good were they? And the premonitions, who did they serve? A gift or even a curse serves a purpose, but I cannot think of any instance in my life where that was true. *Yes, you can Lynn. Stop this.*

Sheriff Hill touched me on the shoulder and startled, I almost fell off the boulder into the water.

"I thought everyone was gone," I said.

"Don't sit there second guessing yourself, Lynn. You were not responsible for what happened here today. Bob Wyliff used poor judgment, that's all. We can continue — you still have evidence — use it. Find a way and so will I."

"Who will believe anything I can offer? You have seen the corruption and how widespread it is. What can either of us do now?"

"You have the rope and the duct tape, and now you have my story. Tell it." Sheri's voice whispered. *"I'll take care of the rest."*

Sheriff Hill helped me up off the boulder and hesitating, not knowing what to say to each other, we walked to our cars each lost in thought. I looked back one last time and headed home.

* * * *

Although the visions of Sheri stopped after the dive, my thoughts of her have not. Troubled over my inability to help her, I obsess over what I could have done differently. I watch for updates in the news and wait, hoping someone will come forward with information. They have not.

I know my visions will go on, other people, other places. But none will touch my life or soul as Sheri's did. There are others in this world who share the gift of clairvoyance, and my heart goes out to them. It is a tremendous burden to bear at times, but greatly rewarding when something wondrous comes from it.

I think about the long journey I was allowed to take with Sheri, and I am in awe of the strange and haunting friendship we formed. I question how it is even possible, but mysteries abound in our universe, and maybe we are not meant to understand. The rest of the world wants to know what really happened to Sheri. They disbelieve the FBI. The Internet is inundated with stories, blogs, testimonials, and well wishes for her family. The years are passing but the interest in her case is growing.

FBI Special Agent Arthur, disgraced, broken and crucified by the media, was transferred to another district and assigned a desk job. Sheri's case has become known as one of the most bungled cases in FBI history, and Arthur was responsible.

The governor was convicted of ethics violations and removed from office. The parole board approved his parole, but required a judge or district attorney's signature, and his *friends* refused. Lung cancer painfully deteriorated his body and ended his life.

Sheri's final words ring in my ears. *Those responsible for my demise have much to fear. You will be held accountable for your actions.* I eagerly await the accounting.

District Attorney, Donald Butcher, was informed that his only daughter was killed in a commercial plane crash.

The senior partner joined another law firm, disengaging himself from all past and possibly incriminating associations.

Congressman Wise retired due to a failing heart that eventually killed him. Ironic that the kidnapper, Daniel Spicer suffered from the same affliction.

Cause and effect? Karmic payback? Coincidence? Sheri?

The rope retrieved from the dive contains the same blood type as Sheri's, but it is only a rope stained with blood — inconclusive evidence without tangible facts to support it. I am left with only her story, and I choose to share it with the world in the hopes that those who know the truth will no longer be afraid to step forward. She deserves and has earned your help.

It is mid-September and the hot, humid Georgia air is stifling. Nirvana captures my mind as my eyes become heavy from the heat, and I am instilled with an unusual sense of peace, completeness, a knowing.

* * * *

The doorbell chimed loudly interrupting Larry Noland's Saturday afternoon football game televised on the sports channel.

"Who the hell is that?" he yelled through the room to Noel, his wife of three years.

"I'll get it, Larry," she sweetly said and walked to the front door. It was late autumn and the air nipped at her face as she opened the front door to a pretty, brunette woman. She noticed two black official looking cars parked in the circular driveway.

"Mrs. Noland, is your husband home?" the pretty brunette asked politely.

"Yes, but he's watching the football game. May I help you?"

The woman reached into her left blazer pocket and flashed a badge. A couple of men dressed in dark business suits got out of black cars parked in the driveway and walked to the door.

"Ms. Noland, I'm Special Agent Hobbs FBI. May we come in?"

"What's this all about?" she asked in a shaky voice.

Special Agent Hobbs and the two agents walked through the door past Ms. Noland without waiting for an invitation and looked around the room.

"Nice house. Would you please get your husband?"

"Larry, come in here right now," Ms. Noland said with alarm.

"What do you want? You're making me miss the game," Larry

said irritably as he got up off the sofa and walked into the foyer.

"Larry Noland, I'm Special Agent Hobbs, remember me? I assisted in the investigation of your first wife's kidnapping," she said sternly. "We have a warrant for your arrest for the murder of Sheridan Hilliard Noland." She waved the warrant in his face and tried not to smile. The two agents turned Larry around, handcuffed his hands behind his back and Special Agent Hobbs read him his rights with immense pleasure. She had waited six years for this day.

Larry yelled over her voice. "You can't do this. I didn't kill Sheri. You people don't know when to quit." He frantically tried to free his hands. With pounding heart and gasping breath he pleaded with Special Agent Hobbs, his face drained of color.

Special Agent Hobbs and the two agents escorted Larry out the front door as he yelled back to his wife, "Get Bob Selten. Get my lawyer on the phone now." The second Ms. Noland stood in shock at the doorway while the agents placed Larry into the backseat of one of the cars and drove out of the driveway.

With a start Larry sat up in the middle of his bed, sweat pouring from his forehead. The bed sheets were tangled around his arms, pinning them behind him. He looked around the room with eyes wide and afraid. He shivered but there was no coldness in the room. He looked at the window. Daylight. The clock on the nightstand beside his bed read nine thirty in the morning. He slowly untangled the sheets and looked at his wife asleep beside him.

"Son-of-a-bitch it was a damn dream," he muttered. "It didn't really happen. God, what a nightmare."

Larry shivered again, wiped the sweat from his forehead, got out of bed and walked around the room trying to calm himself. He looked out the window at the beautifully landscaped yard surrounding the driveway just to make sure there were no black cars parked there. He took deep, slow breaths and stood staring, trembling. Larry peered out the window once more, but this time he saw the front yard of his house in Canton, and in the driveway was his

Jeep. He was sure he saw Sheri sitting in the seat with a scarf covering her eyes.

"What the hell?" Shaking his head and rubbing his face, he tried to clear his vision. "I'm hallucinating. What the hell was in those drinks last night?" he said out loud not daring to look out the window again.

With a heavy sigh, Larry turned around and started to the kitchen for coffee still muttering. He stopped in the middle of the room stricken with terror.

Wrapped in a cloak of glowing mist she stood on the far side of the bedroom with an odd, peaceful look on her face. His mouth opened and closed but produced no sound. He heard his new baby softly whimpering from the nursery down the hall. He looked at his wife asleep in their bed not stirring.

I'm still dreaming, he thought and shook his head again trying to wake himself.

Sheri watched him.

He looked into her eyes and fear and guilt crawled over his flesh and into his mind, twisting and distorting his thoughts until he no longer remembered anything except the night he betrayed Sheridan Hilliard Noland. Conscious time ceased to exist for Larry Noland in the morning light of his bedroom. In the final moments of his sanity he heard a soft but chilling voice.

"According to the seed that's sown,
So is the fruit you reap there from,
Doer of good will gather good,
Doer of evil, evil reaps,
Down is the seed and thou shalt taste
The fruit thereof."

(Samyutta Nikaya)

Justice does not always take place in a courtroom.

CPSIA information can be obtained at www.ICGtesting.com
Printed in the USA
LVOW11s1340030814

397271LV00001B/231/P